Trammel stood at his place, smoke coming out of his ears. Beside him, Nimble smirked. He jabbed his finger toward me. "There's your thief!"

Thief. It was always like this. They weren't going to believe me no matter what I said.

Still . . . I knew how thieves worked. If I could get away from all the fuss and *looking after* and the ducal magister box that I didn't fit into, I could get out into the city, and once I was in the city I could sneak and spy and find out who was really stealing the locus magicalicus stones, and deal with the two-magic problem too, if I could find time for it.

Praise for *The Magic Thief*

"A delight to read. The compelling plot is sure to draw avid fans back for more." —*The Bulletin of the Center for Children's Books* (starred review)

"I couldn't put it down. Wonderful, exciting stuff!"
—Diana Wynne Jones,
author of *Howl's Moving Castle*

"A fun read for fans of fantastic adventures."
—*School Library Journal*

"What works wonderfully well here is the boy's irresistible voice."
—ALA *Booklist* (starred review)

"Conn, equally gifted at picking locks and being a thorn in the side of all, remains a vivid, memorable lead." —*Kirkus Reviews*

The MAGIC THIEF

HOME

BOOK FOUR

BY SARAH PRINEAS

ILLUSTRATIONS BY
ANTONIO JAVIER CAPARO

HARPER
An Imprint of HarperCollinsPublishers

Library of Congress Cataloging-in-Publication Data
Prineas, Sarah.
    Home / by Sarah Prineas ; illustrations by Antonio Javier
Caparo. — First edition.
        pages   cm. — (Magic thief ; book 4)
    Summary: "Young wizard's apprentice Connwaer disguises
himself as a chimney swift in order to identify who has been stealing
the locus stones in Wellmet"— Provided by publisher.
    ISBN 978-0-06-220956-6 (pbk.)
    [1. Magic—Fiction.   2. Wizards—Fiction.   3. Apprentices—
Fiction.   4. Fantasy.]   I. Caparo, Antonio Javier, ill.   II. Title.
PZ7.P93646Hom 2014   2014010023
[Fic]—dc23   CIP
                                                                     AC

Typography by Sasha Illingworth
15 16 17 18 19   PC/RRDH   10 9 8 7 6 5 4 3 2 1
❖
First paperback edition, 2015

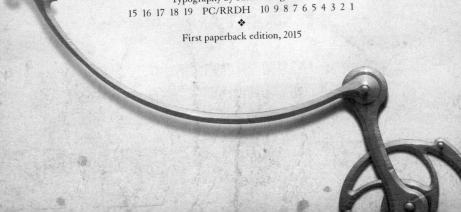

TO
CHARLES COLEMAN FINLAY.
WITHOUT YOUR MENTORSHIP,
SUPPORT, AND FRIENDSHIP,
I WOULD NOT BE A WRITER.
THANKS, CHARLIE.

WELLMET

6

1

7

2

5

8 8

10

3

11

12

8

15

9 13

4

14

S

THE RIVER
1. Heartsease
2. Academicos
3. Wizards' houses
4. Magisters Hall
5. Night Bridge
6. Crowe's hiding place
7. Nimble's house
=== tunnels under
      river to islands

THE TWILIGHT
8. Factories and warehouses
9. Sark Square
10. Dusk House ruins
11. New Dusk House
12. Half Chick Lane
13. Strangle Street
14. Sparks's house
15. Mudlark Kids' Shack

THE SUNRISE
16. Dawn Palace

CHAPTER 1

A thief is nothing like a fine gentleman.

A wizard isn't, either.

"I know who I am, Ro," I said. "And I'm not somebody who goes to meetings."

But there I was in a meeting room, even though I didn't want to be. At least it was mostly empty, just Rowan and me. The room had shiny marble floors, tree-shaped pillars against the walls, and high, arched windows. One of the windows had a stained-glass tree built into it, and when the light from outside came through it, the room turned green. Sitting at the end of the table, with the green light shining over her and making her look a little green herself, was Rowan, my best friend, who happened to be the duchess of our city, Wellmet. She wore a green velvet dress and had her red hair in a braid down her back; she also had on her gold spectacles and an impatient look.

"I know you know who you are," Rowan said crossly. "You are the same Conn you ever were. And," she went on, "I need you to attend this meeting. It's important." She got to her feet and came over to me, where I stood by the door. "All right?"

Before I could say no, a polite little knock interrupted us.

"What is it?" Rowan called.

The door opened and a tall, paper-thin woman

edged into the room. She had on a green dress like Rowan's, but with neat white cuffs and collar, and had her gray hair scraped back into a tight bun. Her mouth was scraped into a tight smile. "Duchess," she said in a scrapy voice, "I am so *exceedingly* sorry to intrude, but it is past time for the meeting to begin. You know how important it is to be punctual."

Rowan sighed. "Yes, all right, I know." She nodded at the woman. "Conn, this is Miss Dimity, my new secretary." She pointed at me. "Miss Dimity, Conn is . . . um . . . a rather special wizard."

Miss Dimity looked me up and down, and her eyes bulged, as if she didn't like what she was seeing. She sniffed and turned to Rowan. "Duchess? May I show them in?"

Rowan said yes, and her councilors and advisors—and a couple of magisters—trooped in. Most of them frowned when they saw me and went to settle in their places at the long table.

"Hello, cousin," said Embre, the Underlord who

ran the Twilight part of the city, as he rolled past me in his wheeled chair. He was a thin young man a bit older than Rowan, dressed in black trousers and coat that matched his black hair.

Rowan, looking duchessly, went to sit at the head of the table.

The chair at her right was empty. She pointed at it—my seat.

Kerrn, the captain of the palace guards, was taking her place at the other end of the table, and she gave me a sharp glance with her ice-chip blue-gray eyes. I knew what she was thinking: *I have got my eye on you, thief.*

Nevery had come in, too, and was smiling and pulling on the end of his beard.

"Won't you sit down?" Rowan said, watching me carefully.

"Ro—" I started.

"Conn," Rowan hissed through gritted teeth. "Sit *down*."

Oh, all right. I walked 'round the table to the

empty chair. Whispers followed me. *Why has the duchess invited him? The gutterboy? What's Nevery's cursed apprentice doing here?*

"Well, boy?" Nevery whispered to me as I slid into my chair.

"Why does she want me here?" I whispered back.

"Hmm," he said, no answer. "You ought to have your locus magicalicus with you. Where is it?"

Pip, he meant. I shrugged. The dragon Pip was about the size of a kitten, but much more fierce. Its true name was Tallennar, but when I wasn't doing magic I called it Pip for a nickname. When I had found my second locus magicalicus stone, Pip had swallowed it, and the stone was still inside it—so now I needed Pip with me if I wanted to do any magic. It was probably off hunting pigeons. It liked to eat them whole, spitting out the feathers.

Beside me, Rowan cleared her throat. "I have called this meeting today for two reasons. One is because, as we are all aware, we now have two magics—magical beings, I should say—settled in our city, a change that I am certain will affect us all in some way. As Magister Brumbee has informed me, there is no precedent for such a thing. Isn't that right, Brumbee?"

"Ah, yes." Brumbee, a plump wizard sitting down the table from me, nodded. "The two, ah, magics. We do not know yet *how* they will work together, or indeed, even *if* they will. A concern, indeed."

On the other side of the table, Magister Trammel leaned forward, scowling. "The two magics are converging over the hospital on the medicos island, and our healing spells are effecting in unexpected ways. Look at this." He pointed at the man sitting next to him. An old, mournful-faced man, wearing a tall black hat. "Just this morning we treated this man for a headache, and look!" Trammel reached over and took off the man's hat. Where his hair should have been, a crop of flowers sprang up, bright yellow and white. The old man nodded sadly, and the flowers bobbed on their long stems.

"Daisies!" Trammel complained. "Sprouting from his head! It's terrible!" He shot me an angry glance.

Another magister, the bat-faced, bat-eared Nimble, spoke up in his whiny voice. "We all know who to blame, too, don't we?"

I slouched lower in my seat. The city had two magics because I was the one who had given the Arhionvar magic a place here, instead of banishing it forever. The magisters blamed me for the upset that occurred when Arhionvar had first arrived: There had been whirlwinds and flaming rocks raining down from the sky, and parts of the Twilight had been burned down or blown away, and the magics still hadn't worked themselves out. They were two huge creatures yoked together, but they were pulling in different directions. I could feel how upset they were—any wizard could feel it if he or she paid attention. It was like an uneasiness in the air, like that moment right before lightning strikes in the middle of a towering thunderstorm.

Was *this* why Ro wanted me at the meeting? So I could listen to the magisters growling about the problem of having two magics in Wellmet?

Brumbee nodded. "The magics are entangled in some way over the academicos, too. Or perhaps *entangled* is not the right word. Overlapping? Linked in some way?" He leaned over to glance at Trammel, down at the other end of the table. "What do you think, Trammel?"

"Completely and incomprehensibly ruined, I should say," Trammel answered sharply.

"Oh, dear," Brumbee said. "*Ruined* is too strong a word, I think. Yet I cannot quite know what to expect whenever I take out my locus magicalicus to do a spell. The apprentice students find it most alarming."

I nodded.

Rowan saw. "You have something to add, Conn?"

Not really. "No," I said. But I'd start working

to figure it out as soon as I could. The magisters were sort of right. I'd given the Arhionvar magic a place here, with the old Wellmet magic, and so the two-magic problem *was* my responsibility. But the two magics were very different from each other. The Wellmet magic was much older, and it felt warm and comforting, but it was weak, too. The Arhionvar magic wasn't evil, it was just much stronger; it felt like a mountain, cold and stony, but it could be like a solid, protecting wall, too. It'd been alone for a long time, searching for a city so it wouldn't be alone anymore. I wasn't sure what I'd have to do to get them both settled here in Wellmet.

Nevery gave me one of his keen-gleam looks.

I know, Nevery. But if I said anything, the magisters would just get angry—angrier—and that wouldn't help anything.

Rowan sighed. "I repeat. I am sure you know more about the magics than anyone here, Conn. You have something to add?"

I sat up straighter. All right. "You know that the magics aren't just"—I shrugged—"not just clouds of magic floating around. They're beings that were once dragons."

"Not everyone agrees with that radical notion," Nimble whiningly interrupted.

"It doesn't matter if you agree with it or not," I shot back. "That's what they are. The magics are huge and powerful. They're drawn to the city because there are people here, and it means they're not alone, and they do want what's best for us, but they can't understand us. We're tiny to them, so tiny they can hardly perceive us individually. Only a wizard with a locus stone can speak to them so that they'll hear." I looked around the table. Most of them were staring and it was clear as clear that they weren't really understanding.

Nevery, though, was nodding. "Go on, Connwaer," he ordered.

"Right, well, we can't control them. I don't know what it means that we have two magics now. They might be twice as powerful. They might work together, or they might not. Everything about the magics could stay the same, or it could change."

Nimble whined about that, and Trammel banged his fist, and Brumbee said, "Oh, dear," and then they argued about the magic problem for a long time, with nothing decided except to form a committee to talk about it some more, and two subcommittees for what they called *related issues.*

This was why I didn't go to meetings.

"And now," said Rowan at last, "the second reason I called today's meeting." She smiled brightly, but she wasn't fooling me. She was nervous. "I'm pleased to inform you all that I am hereby naming Connwaer"—she pointed at me—"the new ducal magister."

I sat up straight in my chair. *What?*

"What!" shouted Trammel, leaping to his feet. "That gutterboy?"

"Unthinkable!" shouted Nimble from across the

table, and the councilors and advisors exclaimed and shook their heads.

"Oh, dear." Magister Brumbee wrung his hands and looked worriedly 'round the table. "Oh, dear me."

My cousin Embre was grinning across at me, his black eyes sparkling. Rowan sat there looking duchessly, waiting for the bubbling and boiling to die down.

Beside me, Nevery was smiling.

"You knew she was going to do this," I accused.

His smile broadened. "It's a very great honor, boy," he said, speaking loudly to be heard over the noise.

A very great *honor*, he called it? Not likely. The ducal magister was the most powerful wizard in the city. That wasn't so bad, but the ducal magister had to wear fancy clothes and go to lots of boring meetings, and he had to live in gold-encrusted rooms in the Dawn Palace instead of at home where he belonged.

If I was the ducal magister, the other wizards would *always* look at me funny; they'd never trust me—as far as they were concerned, I was either a gutterboy thief or I was the dangerously radical wizard they blamed for the two-magic problem.

At the head of the table, Rowan raised her hand, and after a few moments the people around the table quieted down. "I can see there is some concern—" she began, and the hubbub boiled up again.

Right at that moment, I heard a *tap-tap-tap* at one of the tall windows. Pip, back from hunting pigeons, wanting to come in out of the rain.

I got up and opened the window. In a whirl of golden wings and emerald-green scales, Pip tumbled into the room, shedding raindrops. Catching the air with its wings, it flapped to the table and landed in the middle of it, lashing its tail.

All of the magisters and councilors and advisors stopped talking and stared.

Then, its claws leaving scratches on the shiny tabletop, Pip crawled over to my place. It fixed me with an ember-bright red eye, opened its mouth, and dropped something on the table in front of me.

A shiny black shard of rock on a golden chain.

"Is that—" Brumbee said, craning his neck to look.

"A locus stone!" exclaimed Trammel.

Brumbee peered more closely at it. "My goodness! That's the locus stone of my apprentice, Keeston. It went missing last night!"

I recognized it, too. Without thinking, I reached out and picked it up.

The other wizards at the table gasped; Brumbee ducked behind his raised arms. Beside me, Nevery snatched up his cane and leaped to his feet.

The stone and its length of chain lay in my hand. I felt a buzz from it, a tingling that ran up my finger bones and itched in the bones of my arm.

I shouldn't have been able to touch someone else's stone at all. True, I'd stolen Nevery's locus stone when I'd been a pickpocket gutterboy, and the stone hadn't killed me, but that'd been strange enough that he'd taken me on as his apprentice afterward. Anybody else in the city would die if they touched a wizard's locus magicalicus. Even a wizard would die if he or she touched another wizard's locus stone.

That meant if this stone had gone missing, only one person in the city could have taken it.

The other magisters knew this. They were all staring at me, and Captain Kerrn at the other end of the table was glaring, and it was clear as clear what they were thinking.

Thief.

CHAPTER 2

"**T**hief!" Magister Trammel shouted, jumping to his feet, jabbing a finger at me. "You see? He is not fit to be the ducal magister! Captain Kerrn, arrest him!"

Kerrn stalked around the table toward me.

I did what any thief would do when somebody accuses him of stealing something—whether he's stolen the thing or not. I dropped

Keeston's locus stone and ducked under the table, scrambled to where Embre's thin legs hung down, and poked my head out.

"Conn?" I heard Embre say.

There, the door. I crawled from under the table and went quick-dart out the door and down the hallway, my running footsteps echoing on the marble floor. Pip shot after me.

From behind, Kerrn burst from the meeting-room door. "Stop him!" she shouted. At the other end of the hall, two guards stepped out, blocking my way.

Drats! I skidded to a stop, and Pip flew past me, then banked with a flutter of wings and dropped onto my shoulder, gripping my sweater with its claws. I whirled back, and Kerrn was there, scowling.

My heart was thump-bumping in my chest, and I backed away from her.

No, wait.

I was *not* the ducal magister but I was a wizard with a dragon locus stone, so she couldn't grab me by the collar and slam me against a wall. Still, I could tell she wanted to. She clenched her fists and made a sound in the back of her throat that sounded like *grrrr*.

Behind Kerrn, Rowan stuck her head out of the meeting-room door. "Did you catch him?" Seeing me, she came all the way out. "My office, Captain Kerrn, and you too, Connwaer," she ordered. "Now."

"Yes, Duchess Rowan," Kerrn answered, without taking her eyes from me. She put her hand on the pommel of her sword. "Will you come?"

I backed up a step. On my shoulder, Pip lashed its tail.

"Or do I put you in chains first?" Kerrn growled.

Oh, all right. "I'll come," I said.

In her office, Rowan sat behind the desk and an angry-looking Nevery was just sitting down beside Embre, who was in his wheeled chair. The office was crowded with lace-doilied chairs and dusty trees in pots, and piles of books and papers.

"Duchess Rowan," Kerrn said, and gave me a

push. "Here is the ducal magister." She said *ducal magister* the way she might say *poisonous viper*.

"I'm not the—" I started, before Rowan silenced me with a sharp glare.

"Thank you, Captain," she said, and gazed at me over her golden spectacles. For a moment she reminded me of her mother. "Sit, Connwaer," she said, pointing at the other padded chair before her desk.

Instead of going to sit there I stayed by the door, leaning against the wall with my hands in my pockets. Pip dropped off my shoulder, then flapped across the room to the windowsill, where it crouched watching us, its eyes glowing red like coals in a winter hearth. Raindrops ticked against the windowpanes outside.

Before anybody said anything, there was a loud knocking at the door; it opened and Rowan's secretary, Miss Dimity, poked her head in. "Duchess Rowan—" she whispered.

"What is it?" Rowan asked, straightening.

"I'm so *very, very* sorry to interrupt, but several council members are demanding to see you, Your Grace. They insist that the, um"—she bulged her eyes at me, and it was clear as clear that she wasn't seeing a *ducal magister*—"that this young person should be arrested for thievery."

"Duchess Rowan?" Kerrn said, waiting for orders.

At her desk, Rowan shook her head. "Oh, curse them, anyway," she said with a sigh. "Tell them to wait, Miss Dimity." The secretary nodded and went out. Rowan frowned at me. "You'll have to do something about this thieving dragon of yours, Connwaer."

"Pip's not a thief," I said.

"Really," Rowan said, her voice dry.

Well, Pip was a thief. Its true name, Tallennar, meant *thief* in the dragon language. But it wouldn't steal locus stones. Would it? Maybe it would. It had stolen my locus stone and swallowed it. But why steal Keeston's stone?

Rowan was shaking her head. "It's not exactly

an auspicious start to your term as ducal magister."

"Ro, I'm not the ducal magister," I said.

"Yes, you are," Rowan insisted.

"No, I'm not," I insisted right back at her.

"All right then, Conn." Rowan leaned forward and put her elbows on the desk. "You said you know who you are. So tell me." She waved around the room at Embre and Kerrn and Nevery. "Tell all of us. Who are you?"

That was easy. "I'm Nevery's apprentice."

Nevery shook his head. "You know more about the magical beings than I do, boy."

That was true. "I'm a wizard, then," I said.

"The other magisters don't think so," Rowan said. "They think you're a troublemaker."

Drats, that was true, too.

"Once a thief, always a thief," Kerrn put in.

"I'm not a thief," I shot back.

"Well, then?" Rowan said, sitting back and looking satisfied, as if she'd proven something. "What are you?"

I glared at her.

"You see?" she said. "I'm right. And I think that will be all," she said. "Conn, you stay for a moment." She nodded at Nevery. "Magister Nevery, will you settle the magisters?"

"If they can be settled." Nevery got up from his chair. "Which I doubt." He bristled his eyebrows at me. "We'll discuss this further when you get home to Heartsease, Connwaer."

I shrugged. He could talk if he wanted to. I didn't have any more to say about it.

"Well, boy?" Nevery asked sharply.

I glanced up at him. He was studying me with his keen-gleam black eyes.

I knew what he was thinking. Not very long ago, when I had tied the two magics to Wellmet, the magics had taken what was me, but left my body behind. For a long time I'd been lost, like a walking, talking puppet-boy. Ever since I'd found myself again, Nevery had been keeping a closer eye on me. Maybe he thought I would disappear again if he wasn't paying attention.

"You'll come straight home, my lad?" he asked.

"Yes, Nevery," I said, because I knew it would make him not worry.

Nevery nodded, then strode from the room, his cane going *tap-tap* on the stone floor.

Embre smiled at Rowan. "You'll keep me informed?" he asked her. He leaned forward and brushed the back of Rowan's hand with his fingers.

She blushed, then jerked her hand away and gave him an annoyed nod. "Of course, Underlord."

Captain Kerrn followed Embre as he wheeled himself out. Sure as sure Kerrn would wait outside the door, then hustle me out of the Dawn Palace when Rowan was done with me.

The office door clicked closed.

Just me and Rowan. My best friend. Who wanted me to be someone I really couldn't be.

A *tappity-tap* on the door. "Duchess Rowan?" Miss Dimity. "I *implore* you to forgive me for inter-rupting," the secretary said. "But I must remind you, Your Grace, that according to our daily agenda, it is time for you to change into your formal gown for this evening's musical gala."

"Yes, I'm coming," Rowan answered. "I just need a moment. Please wait outside."

"You don't want to be late, Your Grace," Miss Dimity reminded, and with a sniff, went out and closed the door.

Rowan blew out a sigh. "Musical gala. It'll be harps again, I expect." She turned briskly to me. "Look, Conn, I know you're happy as you are, and I really am sorry to insist, but the ducal magister has to be you."

"Why?" I asked.

She was barely holding on to her patience, I could tell. "It has to do with power," she said. "The duchess, the Underlord, and the ducal magister. We each do our jobs and the city stays . . ." She held her hands palm up. "Balanced. Do you understand?"

I understood that, but why me? "Nevery'd be better at it."

Rowan took off her golden spectacles and tossed them onto her desk. Then she came 'round and flopped into one of the padded chairs. She glanced at me, then studied the tips of her black shoes. "Conn, I've been training all my life to become duchess of this city. I've had lessons in swordcrafting, diplomacy, government, budget management, etiquette, architecture, city planning, and in magic. But"—her voice quavered a little—"my mother died before she should have. I'm the duchess, but I'm only sixteen years old." She sat up straight and pointed in the direction of the Twilight, where my cousin Embre, the Underlord, lived. "And Embre is nineteen. Both of us are very young for our positions. Nevery is much older and very powerful."

And so he threw off the balance. I got it.

Rowan pointed at me. "You, on the other hand, don't overbalance me and Embre. You're the right age, and, like us, you're still discovering the reach of your power. It has to be you. *Especially* now, with the magics settled here so precariously."

I didn't think she was right about that. I didn't say anything.

"And, well," Rowan went on, looking at the tips of her shoes again. "I'm so busy right now, trying to become a good duchess, as my mother was. I work all the time and it's—well, it's lonely." She gave a tired sigh. "You're my friend. I want you here."

Maybe, even with all that training she'd done, and even though she was good at it, she didn't like being the duchess. Still, I couldn't be the ducal magister, not even if saying no to Rowan made my heart hurt a little.

It wasn't just about not wanting to go to meetings or live in the fancy rooms in the Dawn Palace. I could do those things if I had to, even if I didn't like them. The problem was that *ducal magister* was a title, but it wasn't what I *was*. Too much of me was still gutterboy; too many of my ideas were too dangerous for the other wizards to understand; too many people didn't trust me, for a lot of reasons, and Nevery was right that I wasn't really his apprentice anymore. I wasn't sure exactly what I was—what my role in Wellmet was supposed to be. But *ducal magister* was not it.

Pip had crawled up the wall to hang upside down on the ceiling, where it puffed out smoke like a little teakettle. "Come on," I called to the little dragon, and turned away.

"Conn!" Rowan called after me.

I didn't answer, but I slammed the office door behind me.

No, it meant. No.

After Kerrn followed me to the front doors of the Dawn Palace, her eyes drilling little eye-shaped holes in my back, I headed out into the wide, puddled streets of the Sunrise. Pip didn't mind the rain, so it hopped off my shoulder and

flew ahead, perching on a step or a sign over a shop doorway, watching me, then flying ahead again.

I went along to the Night Bridge, then to the wizards' tunnels, going down the slippery-steepery steps to the first gate. In the chilly darkness, I leaned against the tunnel wall with my hands in my pockets, waiting for Pip. All around, I could hear the faint *rush-rush* of the river, and the sound of water dripping. After a while, Pip came crawling along the tunnel ceiling. *"Lothfalas,"* I said, the light spell, and the little dragon started to glow. It dropped from the ceiling and landed with a splat in a puddle.

"Tired?" I asked, picking Pip up and holding it up to the gate. I said the opening spell. Giving me a cross-eyed look, Pip put its snout against the lock, which clicked open. We went through all the gates until we got to the last gate that led to Heartsease. Pip opened the lock, then flopped out of my hands to the stone floor of the tunnel.

I grinned down at Pip. "It's your own fault, if

you really did spend the afternoon thieving," I said to it.

Pip burped out another swirl of sparks. The lothfalas spell wore off, and the tunnel went dark.

Shaking my head, I climbed the stairs. At the top, I stopped. Way across the cobbled courtyard, Heartsease was waiting. Home.

When I'd settled the two magics in the city, Heartsease—the house I lived in with Nevery and his bodyguard, Benet—had had its roof blown off. Not for the first time, either. So now the top floor was being rebuilt. Most of it was done, but the cobblestoned courtyard in front of the house was scattered with piles of bricks and barrels of nails, and a huge pile of roofing slates.

It was a narrow building, five stories tall. Each story had three windows across, and the ones on the first floor—the kitchen—were bright with lights, and so were the ones on the next floor up—Nevery's study. His workroom and bedroom were on the third floor, the ground floor was the storeroom and

Benet's room, and the top floor, the one without the finished roof, was mine. I started toward it. Maybe Benet was making pot pie for dinner. Mmm, the kind with gravy and a biscuit crust.

From behind me came the faintest *skff-skff* of footsteps sliding over cobblestones. I felt a prickle on the back of my neck, like I was being watched. I stopped. Rain pattered down. A sooty mist crept along the ground. I glanced over my shoulder. Nothing, just the dark river and the faint lights of the Twilight beyond it.

When I turned back, a man-shaped shadow stood between me and the safe, warm windows of Heartsease.

"This him?" a deep voice asked.

"It is," a deeper voice said from behind me.

I opened my mouth to shout for Pip, when a fist crashed into my face. "Pip!" I gasped out. I staggered back and the man behind me caught me, spun me around, and punched me hard in the ribs.

Then he grabbed me by the front of my sweater.

"You're coming with us, wizard boy."

Oh, no, I wasn't. I gave him a sharp kick in the shins and tried to squirm out of his grip.

He pulled back his fist to hit me again, and I felt Pip coming, a sharp bolt of fire, and then the little dragon was there, shooting like a golden arrow from the mouth of the tunnel and into the face of the man. He dropped me with a muffled shout and raised his hands to defend himself.

I fell onto the hard cobblestones, black spots whirling in front of my eyes. Over my head I heard Pip hissing and spitting puffs of flame, and the men trying to fight the dragon off.

A spell—I needed a spell to keep the men from dragging me away with them. I gasped out the first few words of the embero spell—it was all I could think of and it would change the attackers into animals—when one of the men whirled away from Pip and kicked me in the ribs. I gasped and grabbed at his foot, and as he tumbled down Pip was on him, its claws raking at the man's face.

As the man lumbered to his feet, I scrambled away and Pip hovered over my head, its wings flapping furiously.

The two men, hulking shadows in the darkness, backed away from us. "Curst dragon," I heard one of them mutter.

"We can't get 'im now," the other one said back. "Let's go." And they faded into the darkness and were gone.

My head spun, the excitement of the fight faded, and I tipped over and found myself sprawling on the ground. Cold from the courtyard cobblestones seeped into my bones. Pip landed next to me and stalked around, hissing and lashing its tail. From where I lay I could see the warm lights from the kitchen windows.

Right. Well, it could've been worse if Pip hadn't come. Slowly I creaked up until I was sitting. I pulled up my knees and folded my arms on them, then rested my aching head on my arms. My face hurt and I could feel the blow I'd gotten spreading into a bruise. Blood leaked from my nose and split lip and onto the sleeve of my sweater. Nothing broken though, I didn't think.

Pip crawled up my leg, then onto the top of my head, clinging to my hair.

"Ow," I said. My voice was muffled in my sweater-sleeve. I shivered, getting cold. Pip hopped down to perch on my shoulder, then edged closer, curling its tail around my neck.

"*Minnervas*," I said, a spell.

The minnervas was supposed to be a warming spell.

But the magisters were right about one thing—the two magics were not working the way they were supposed to.

As the spell effected, Pip started to glow, which felt nice at first, but then the spell went wrong and its warmth turned hotter until its belly burned red-hot, and I was dizzily scrambling to my feet while pushing Pip off my shoulder.

Ow. I rubbed at the burned spot on my sweater.

On the ground, Pip snapped at its belly, which glowed like a hot stove on a winter day. Quickly I stopped the minnervas spell. Pip glared at me.

"Sorry," I whispered, and shook my aching head, trying to think.

Right, the magics were a problem, I knew that already. They really were like two dragons, both trying to fit into one dragon's space, and even a simple spell like the minnervas was enough to make them twitchy.

But now those men had tried to kidnap me. *Wizard boy*, they'd called me. Who were they? What was going on? Why did they want me?

And were they going to try again?

CHAPTER 4

Getting across the courtyard took a long time because I had to keep waiting with my eyes closed until my head stopped spinning, and then going on without tripping over a pile of

lumber or extra bricks.

I needed to get upstairs without Nevery and Benet seeing me and making a fuss. And I needed time to think.

I had been a thief; I was good at sneaking. I crept into Heartsease and up the stairs, past the kitchen, where I heard Benet clattering pans on the stove. A stair creaked.

"That you?" Benet called. Like Nevery, since I'd been lost and then found again, Benet wanted to know where I went and that I'd gotten home safely.

I coughed, and kept my voice steady. "Yes, it's me," I answered.

"Dinner soon," he said.

I kept going up the stairs, past Nevery's study, where I didn't hear anything, and up to my room.

Before putting on a light I paused, wondering if the spell would work. Steadying myself and closing my eyes, I reached out and sensed the magics. They felt more settled now. Maybe they'd been twitchy before because Pip had been defending me from those kidnappers. Might as well try it. "*Lothfalas*," I whispered, and Pip breathed out a puff of light that drifted across the room and settled in a glass-globed lantern on a shelf.

On one side of the room I had my worktable, boxes of books that I hadn't unpacked yet, a high stool, and bare wooden floors. A ladder leaned against one wall, and there was a pile of broken roof slates next to it. On the other side of the room was my bed with another box of books beside it, the fireplace, a warm red rug that was still rolled up, and a box of clothes. Everything had a coating of sawdust on it, and overhead the roof was half finished and half canvas stretched over wooden beams. It was enough to keep the rain and damp out, mostly. It was home, completely.

Leaving the lantern on the shelf, I creaked over to the bed and lay down on top of the blankets. Pip curled on the pillow next to me, one of its claw-paws resting against my face. I let the light go out and closed my eyes.

After a while I heard heavy footsteps coming up

the stairs. From outside the door, down a couple of steps, Benet called, "Dinner."

In the dark I dragged myself off the bed and over to the door and opened it a crack. "I'm not hungry, Benet," I said. The words came out stiffly because of my split lip.

I held my breath until I heard him grunt, then stomp away, down the stairs.

I went back to bed.

After a short while, I heard other footsteps on the stairs. Nevery. He knocked on the door, then pushed it open.

As he muttered the lothfalas spell, kindling a light, I pushed Pip away and pulled the pillow over my head.

"Don't be ridiculous, boy," Nevery said. "Of course you're hungry. You're *always* hungry. Come down now; I want to talk to you about being the ducal magister, and about this locus-stone-stealing dragon of yours."

"I'm just going to sleep," I said, from under the pillow.

Nevery stopped. "Something's wrong," he said.

Just go away, Nevery.

His footsteps came across the room, and then he lifted the pillow off my head.

I cracked open my eye, the one that wasn't swollen shut, to see. He stared at me, his face turning to chipped stone. "Who did this?" His voice was low and angrier than I'd ever heard it, and I knew he wasn't angry at me.

Heavy footsteps from the stairs interrupted us. "Here, you lot," Benet said, coming in the doorway. "Dinner's getting cold." Then he saw me.

"A fight?" Nevery asked me.

Benet bulled across the room, then stared down at me, his burly arms crossed. "No. That's professional work, that is. Who?" he asked.

"It's not so bad," I said, sitting up stiffly. I'd had the fluff beaten out of me before; it really wasn't.

"It's bad enough, boy," Nevery said.

Benet came closer, peering into my face. "You tell who did this. Now."

All right. "I don't know who did it." Drats, they needed to know more than that. I looked up at Nevery and tried not to shiver so he wouldn't see how scared I'd been. "They were waiting for me. Outside in the courtyard." I didn't mention that the men had tried to kidnap me. I knew they'd worry even more if they found out about that part of it.

"Curse it," Nevery growled.

Benet clenched his fists and looked ready to squeeze the life out of the fluff-beaters if he got his hands on them. "What did they want?" he asked.

"I don't know," I answered.

"It can't be a coincidence." Nevery narrowed his eyes and studied me. "A locus stone stolen and now this. What are you up to, boy?"

"Nothing, Nevery!" I protested.

"It must be something," he growled.

No, really! I wasn't up to anything!

During the night I woke up sure as sure that the two men were lurking by the door of my room.

Shivering, I sat up and stared into the shadows, listening for the *skff-skff* of stealthy footsteps and waiting for a heavy fist to come crashing out of the dark.

Instead, all I heard were raindrops pattering on the canvas overhead.

Why had those men been after me?

Then I felt Pip curled against my side and the Wellmet magic's warmth and Arhionvar's stony protection wrapped around me. I *was* safe, even if those fluff-beaters wanted me to think I wasn't. Knowing that, I closed my eyes and went back to sleep without any more dark dreams.

BENET'S TO-DO LIST

Talk to Fist and Hand about professionals working out of the Twilight.

Beat the fluff out of professionals, if found.

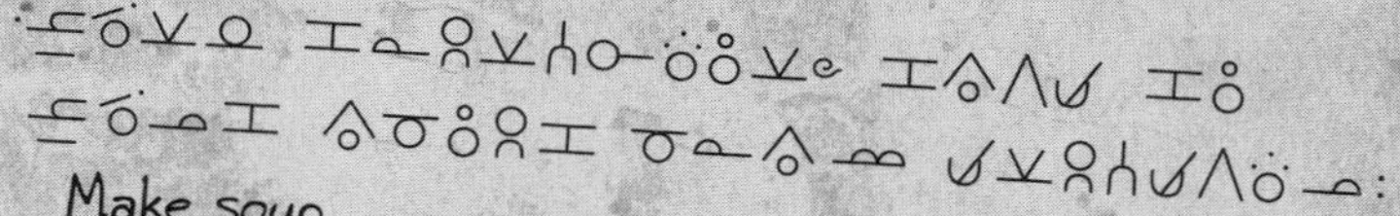

ᚷᚖᐯᚐ � ᚷᚐᚖᐯᚋᚐᚖᚖᐯᚲ ᐯᚐᐱᚗ ᚿᚖᚖᚐᚢ ᚿᚖᚗᐱ ᚐᚢᚖᚖᚐᚢ ᚷᚐᚖᚘᚐ ᚢᐯᚖᚺᐱᚘᐱᚖᚐᚐ:

Make soup.

Bake biscuits.

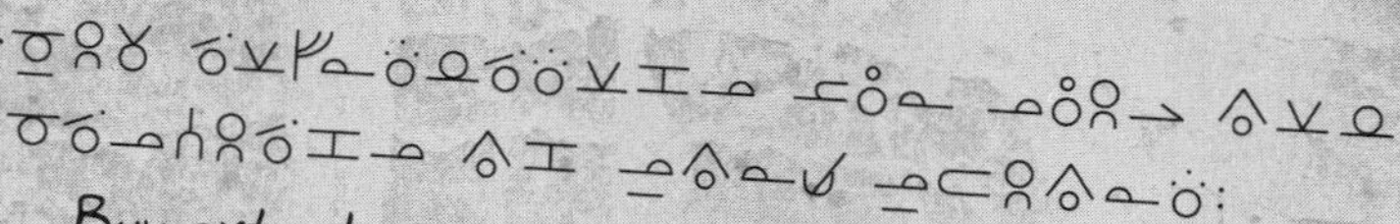

ᚷᚖᚖ ᚖᐯᐱᚖᚖᚖᚖᚖᐯᚿᚐ ᚷᚖᚐ ᚐᚖᚖᚢ ᚐᐯᚐ ᚖᚖᚐᚐᚺᚖᚖᚿᚐ ᚐᚿ ᚐᚖᚐᚢ ᚐᚲᚖᚐᚐᚖ:

Buy extra bacon.

Fix stovepipe.

Bake the scones with berries that Kerrn likes and take them to guard barracks at Dawn Palace.

Buy fingering yarn (blue?), four double pointed needles. Knit socks.

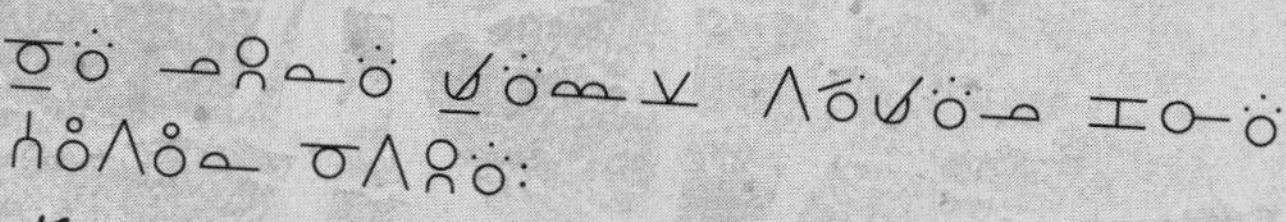

ᚷᚖ ᚐᚖᚐᚖ ᚢᚖᚖᐯ ᐱᚖᚘᚖᚐ ᚿᚐᚖ ᚺᚖᐱᚖᚐ ᚖᐱᚖᚖ:

Keep a closer eye on the kid and his lizard.

CHAPTER 5

The kidnappers had scared me, but I was *not* going to crawl into a hole and hide. I had things to do out in the city. At the meeting the day before, the magisters had been complaining about the instability of the two magics. I

thought maybe it was getting worse, too, because I was more sensitive to what the magics were doing than anyone, and I hadn't noticed it being so bad before.

As I'd told the magisters at the meeting, there was no knowing how the two magics would work together. They might not. If they settled peacefully and worked together, they'd be hugely powerful. But now they were struggling, pushing and pulling at each other, entangled over the city, and it felt like they were on the edge of panic.

I needed to figure out how to help the two magics. And I couldn't do that from my safe, cozy room in Heartsease.

Going out into the city to deal with the magics meant the kidnappers might come after me again. But I wasn't a defenseless gutterboy anymore. I was a wizard, and I needed to come up with some spells to protect myself. Spells that would work in the middle of a fight. If the magics worked, that is.

I got up and, leaving Pip to snooze in the blankets, fetched a couple of old grimoires off the bookshelves, carried them over to the table, and got to work, squinting with my good eye at the pages.

Hmmm.

Magic spells were really the language of the magical beings—the dragon language. Most wizards didn't know much of the spell language, but one thing I was very good at, besides lock picking and thievery, was remembering, so I could hear a magical spell once and repeat it back exactly. That meant I understood the magics' language and I could speak directly to them. Really, any wizard could do it, too, if they thought about it, but none of them had ever tried it.

I thought through all the spellwords I knew. The new spells would need to be short, just a few words so I'd have time to say them if somebody was coming after me. Something like the lothfalas spell, but more focused. I paged through the grimoires until I found a white-bright-light spell, and changed some of the words.

"Come here, Pip," I said. The little dragon snorted in its sleep and didn't move, so I went over to the bed and put my hand on the smooth spot between its wings; then I said the new dazzler spell.

As the spell effected, Pip burst from the blankets, its eyes wide and whirling; a gout of white-bright sparks flashed from its mouth and slammed into my eyes. Then the dragon scrambled with sharp claws up my front and onto my hair, spitting out more sparks as it crouched there.

Squinting through the sparks, I saw its tail lashing before my eyes. Whoops. More proof that the magics were unsettled. Poor Pip!

The little dragon hopped down from my head and crouched in the blankets, still lashing its tail. "Sorry," I said. It gave me a glary glance and curled itself up to go back to sleep.

As tricksy as the magics were, I still thought the spell would work to blind an attacker for a few moments. After a while, the sparks faded and

I could see again. I rubbed my good eye and read some more, figuring out a spell that would prick somebody all over with needles if he tried hitting me. No need to try that one out—I didn't want to prickle myself, or Pip.

There. I felt safer already. But I really did need to go out into the city to get a better feel for what was going on with the magics.

See? I wanted to tell Rowan. *I don't have time for meetings and ducal magistering. I have more important things to do.*

Trying to be careful of my bruised ribs, I put on my black sweater and my coat. I picked up sleeping Pip and put it on my shoulder.

As I slunk down the stairs past Nevery's study, I met Benet coming up.

"Here, you," he said. "Where're you off to?"

I shrugged and tried to edge past him. Important wizard business. No fuss, if you please.

"No you don't," Benet growled, and grabbed me by the arm; he opened the door to Nevery's study and dragged me inside.

Nevery was sitting in his usual chair; standing around the table were Magister Brumbee, looking plump-rumpled and worried, and Magister Nimble, the bat-faced wizard who didn't like me. What were *they* doing here?

Benet let me go. "Caught him sneaking out, sir," he said.

"I wasn't sneaking," I said. Not really. Only a little.

Nevery gave me a narrow-eyed look. "Going out? Where?"

I shrugged. If I told him what I was up to, he'd worry, and I didn't want that.

"*And* he hasn't had his breakfast yet," Benet said from beside me, and folded his arms.

Oops. Very suspicious, me sneaking out before breakfast. "I won't be gone for very long." I glanced at Benet, then at Nevery, and they were both scowling. Brumbee looked even more fretful; Nimble just looked smug, as if he knew something I didn't. "What's the matter?" I asked.

"Hmm," Nevery growled. "Brumbee and

Nimble have just brought the news. Another locus stone has been stolen."

What? "Whose?" I asked.

"Mine!" Magister Nimble said in his whiny voice. "And I know who stole it!"

Oh, no. I knew what he was going to say. "It wasn't me," I said quickly.

"Connwaer." Nevery was giving me his most keenly-gleaming look. "What has your dragon been up to?"

I glanced aside at Pip, asleep on my shoulder. "Nothing, Nevery."

"Oh, dear," Brumbee said.

"Are you certain, boy?" Nevery asked.

"Sure as sure, Nevery," I said. "Pip's been with me all night. It wasn't out stealing Nimble's locus stone. We had nothing to do with it." I held my breath. He *had* to believe me.

Nevery nodded. "Well then," he said, turning to Brumbee and Nimble. "You will have to look else-where for your thief. It wasn't Conn."

"He's lying!" Nimble shrieked.

Nevery got loomingly to his feet, gray and threatening as a stormcloud. He glared thunder and lightning at Nimble. "Conn does not lie."

Nimble gulped and went wide-eyed and silent; Brumbee wrung his hands and muttered his usual *oh dear me*'s.

"Now," Nevery said, still glowering. "Go away."

I ducked out of Benet's grip and headed for the door.

"Not *you*, boy," Nevery said, using his exasperated voice. "Them." He pointed.

Benet opened the door, and the magisters scuttled out and down the stairs.

Nevery settled behind his desk again and looked me up and down. "Trouble, and somehow you're in the thick of it again. I don't know what to do with you, boy."

"You don't have to do anything, Nevery," I said. On my shoulder, Pip woke up and puffed out a cloud of smoke.

"Have a word with the captain," Benet said, from behind me.

"Ah. A very good idea, Benet. I shall. Fetch my hat, cloak, and cane."

"Yes, sir," Benet said, and left the room.

A word with the captain, Benet had said. "A word with Captain Kerrn?" I asked. "Why?"

Nevery glanced at me from under his bushy eyebrows, but didn't answer. Instead he got to his feet and went to the door. Benet met him on the stairs and handed him his things.

Benet gave me a buttered biscuit.

"Come along, boy," Nevery said, putting on his wide-brimmed hat.

"Where're we going?" I asked. I put the biscuit into my coat pocket. Pip cocked its head, as if it was waiting to see what Nevery would say.

Nevery said something in a low voice to Benet, then put on his cloak and swept-stepped down the stairs. "You'll see when we get there," he said.

Oh. I followed Nevery down the stairs and out into the cobbled courtyard. The rain had stopped, but the sky was thick with gray clouds, and a morning fog hovered over the river, making the Twilight and the Sunrise banks invisible. Brown leaves covered the big tree in the middle of the courtyard, and a few black-and-white birds perched in the highest branches, like lookouts.

I dodged a pile of roof slates and ran a couple of steps to catch up to Nevery. "Why are you going to have a word with Kerrn?" I asked.

"You will be living in the Dawn Palace. Captain Kerrn must be told to keep an eye on you."

"Nevery!" I protested. That was a terrible idea. Kerrn hated me! She'd put a guard on my every move! And I was *not* going to live in the Dawn Palace.

"Listen, boy," Nevery growled. "We've got locus stone thefts and a crowd of idiot magisters who think you are the thief. Something is going on, and you're involved in it, somehow." He swirled to a stop. "*And* there's this attack," he said, pointing at my bruised face. He lowered his voice, as if talking to himself. "I will not lose you again, Connwaer." Then he glowered at me from under his bushy eyebrows. "If it means sending you away from Heartsease, then so be it."

Nevery kept a keen eye on me as we crossed the bridge and headed to the Dawn Palace, which sat at the top of the hill like a huge, pink-frosted cake. A chill wind from the river followed us, ruffling my hair and making Nevery's cloak swirl around him. We crunched down the drive and up the wide front stairs, where two palace guards stopped us. We waited just inside the door while one of them went to fetch Rowan.

"I hate this, Nevery," I growled.

"It's to keep you safe, boy," he growled back.

To me, *safe* meant *never doing anything interesting*.

At the sound of footsteps, I looked up. Rowan, followed by Miss Dimity, who carried a stack of papers.

Seeing my bruised face, Rowan's eyes widened. "Oh, Conn!" she said.

"It looks worse than it is," I said.

She stepped closer and put her hand to my cheek. "It looks awful. What happened?"

I shrugged and listened as Nevery told her about the attackers in the courtyard outside Heartsease. "He'll be safer in the Dawn Palace," Nevery said.

Rowan gave me a quick hug. "Yes, we'll take good care of you here, Conn. Miss Dimity has arranged the ducal magister's rooms, so they are all ready for you. I haven't had time to see them, but she says they are quite splendid." She and Nevery turned and set off down the hallway, followed by the secretary. "I'll assign servants to look after you, too, Conn."

I scowled, trailing behind them. I still hadn't agreed to be the ducal magister. And I didn't need *looking after*.

"Excuse me, Your Grace, Magister," Miss Dimity interrupted then.

She was very good at interrupting, I'd noticed.

Rowan paused at the bottom of a wide, carpeted staircase. "What is it?"

"I *do* apologize *most* sincerely, but you have a

meeting now with the stonemasons league."

"Isn't that tomorrow?" Rowan asked impatiently.

"No indeed," Miss Dimity said, and her eyes bulged. "See here, on the agenda." She waved a sheet of paper.

"Yes, of course." Rowan turned to me. "Conn, I have to attend this meeting, but Miss Dimity will show you your rooms, all right?"

No, it wasn't all right. I glared at her.

"You must hurry, Your Grace," Miss Dimity put in. "It simply wouldn't do to keep them waiting."

Rowan closed her eyes for just a moment. "I don't have time for this," she muttered. Opening her eyes, she said, "Will you just *go*, Conn?"

Yes, all right. I gave her the slightest nod. She whirled and snatched the pages that Miss Dimity shoved into her hands and then hurried away down the hall.

"You seem to be well settled, my lad," Nevery said to me. He rested a hand on my shoulder. "As it happens, I have a meeting to attend as well, so I must be going."

It didn't matter what I said, because clear as clear he wasn't going to listen to me, any more than Rowan had. So I stayed quiet.

Nevery shot me one last *behave yourself* look and left.

"Well then!" Miss Dimity said, and scraped her lips into something that was supposed to be a smile, but wasn't really. "Come along."

She led me up a wide stairway, then down a long, carpeted hall to a set of double doors with bronze handles and what looked like a puzzle lock. Tricky to pick a lock like that.

Miss Dimity threw the doors open. "The ducal magister's chambers," she announced.

The main room was very fancy, a study with a few knobbly-looking wooden chairs and wobbly small tables with lace doilies on them, a patterned rug on the floor, and lots of shelves covered with more lace doilies and fancy dishes and silver statues instead of books.

"You see?" Miss Dimity pointed at the walls, where gilt-framed oil paintings of old men and women hung. "The former residents of these rooms, ducal magisters all."

I could tell exactly what she was thinking. A gray-bearded old man or a wrinkly old woman was her idea of a proper ducal magister, not scruffy me.

She was right about that, too.

I stepped farther into the chilly room, looking around. Pip hopped off my shoulder and flapped to one of the high-backed, uncomfortable chairs set next to the hearth. The little dragon landed on the back of the chair, and its claws scratched a gouge in the wood. I glanced over my shoulder to see if Miss Dimity had noticed. She stood near the doorway, watching me with her bulgy eyes. Captain Kerrn had joined her; she said something to the secretary, but kept her eye on me.

Miss Dimity gave me another one of her false smiles. "Do you approve of your rooms, Ducal Magister?"

Not really, no. They were too grand. "I'm not staying here," I said.

Ignoring that, Miss Dimity walked over to

another door and threw it open. "This is your dressing room."

I didn't have enough clothes to need a dressing room.

"Do you see?" She pointed at a row of fancy-fine clothes on hangers, and three brand-new, shiny silk magister's robes. "Magister Nevery says that his manservant is bringing your things."

For some reason, Kerrn's cheeks turned a little pink. "Benet is coming here?"

Miss Dimity's nostrils flared. "If that is his name, yes. But, Ducal Magister," she said grandly to me, "as you can see, you won't need any of your old clothes."

Oh, yes I would. I was *not* going to wear those primp-proper ducal magister robes.

Out in the main room, Miss Dimity glanced at the empty hearth. "Servants will be sent to attend to the fire." She gave a sharp sniff. "Yes, I think that is sufficient." Without another word to me, she hurried out.

I stood in the middle of the room. The frothy

plaster and gilded ceiling arched way above me; the windows stretched up the walls; the empty hearth gaped like a wide mouth; the oil-painted wizards on the walls stared disapprovingly down at me.

Rowan hadn't seen these rooms, but Miss Dimity had told her they were *splendid*. They'd probably make a real ducal magister feel important and powerful.

They made me feel small and cold.

I went over to the window. Drats. The ducal magister's rooms were on the third floor, and there was no ivy growing up past the window, no nearby tree to climb down. I wouldn't be able get out that way when I needed to leave.

When I turned back to the room, I noticed Kerrn still standing in the doorway, hands on her hips. "I know what you are thinking," she said.

She probably did.

She put her hand on the pommel of her sword and spoke like she was giving me an order. "My guards will be watching you. If you wish to go out into the city, you must inform me first, and be accompanied by me or a guard."

Accompanied? Followed and spied on, more likely.

She waited for me to say something. When I didn't, she turned and stalked out of the room, slamming the door behind her.

I looked around the room. It was fancy, but it was a prison, and I was *not* going to stay locked up in it.

Rowan, Duchess of Wellmet,
to Underlord Embre-wing

Magister Nevery just brought Conn to the Dawn
Palace. Apparently Conn was attacked outside
Heartsease. He looks terrible, his face all bruised, and
moving stiffly, as if his ribs hurt. Conn and his dragon
managed to fight off the attackers, but Nevery is
worried—rightly so, I think—that they will try again.

As if that wasn't enough to worry about, my councilors and the magisters remain upset about the stolen
locus stones and the unreliable magics, and want to
blame Conn for all of it. I've just come from a meeting
with several of them, who are insisting that Conn be
arrested and imprisoned—for the good of the city.

I am, as I am sure you must be, quite concerned.
Conn is moving into the ducal magister's rooms in the

Dawn Palace, where he will be under the protection of my guard. I thought it best to keep you informed.

Sincerely,
Rowan, Duchess
Dawn Palace, Wellmet, etc.

PS. I wondered if all in the city seems quite well to you. Apart from this trouble with Conn and the magical beings, have you noticed anything else strange going on?

Rowan—
Anything strange? Why do you ask? Have you?
—Embre

CHAPTER 6

Benet brought my things, clothes, and some equipment from my workroom, and the box of books from beside my bed, but I didn't bother unpacking them except a few of the books. I wouldn't be living in the Dawn Palace for very long.

There was a knock at the door. As I walked across the carpeted floor to open it, Pip leaped from the back of the knobbled chair where it'd been perching and landed on my shoulder. I opened the door. The hallway was dim-dark.

After pausing to check that the magics were calm enough, I said the lothfalas spell, and Pip burped out a puff of pink sparks that floated up to hang over my head. In the glow of the spell, I saw one of Kerrn's guards standing stiff and straight beside the door, and a man wearing green livery, flinching away from the light.

"What?" I said. Pip leaned forward, snorting smoke from its nostrils.

The man edged away, his eyes wide and fixed on Pip. "A, ah—"

"It's not going to hurt you," I said. Pip wasn't, I meant. "What d'you want?"

The man pulled a piece of paper out of his coat pocket. On my shoulder, Pip lashed its tail, and the man jumped back. "A note for the ducal magister," he said quickly. Oh, he was a servant. Still backing away, he held out the paper.

I stepped forward and took it, and the man turned and fled, casting a glance over his shoulder as he went.

The guard beside the door gave me a quick look, checking the bruises on my face, I could see.

"If I go out, are you supposed to follow me?" I asked her.

"To accompany you, yes, Magister," she answered stiffly.

Hmmm.

I went back into the ducal magister's rooms and closed the door. The paper was thick and cream-colored, with Rowan's house crest on it. The handwriting was sloppy, as if she'd been in a hurry when she wrote the note.

Conn, join me for dinner later, just me and some friends. A servant will fetch you. Your dragon is welcome, too. You'll have to tell me what it eats.

—Rowan

⊨ᚦႠ ⅄Ⴍ⊥ ⊥Ⴆ ᓂᱢ
ᐱᲔ⊥ᱢ:

Pip ate pigeons and blackpowder. Sure as sure, Rowan wasn't going to have that at her dining table. Right.

I looked around the room again. It felt like Rowan and Nevery and even Benet were trying to put me into a box that I didn't really fit into. I could feel the walls of the box pressing against me, turning me sort of square-shaped, and I didn't like it.

Well then, I'd better do something about it.

I had two problems facing me. First, figuring out how to settle both magics here in the city. Second, finding out who'd sent the kidnappers and what he or she wanted with me.

Three things, really, because there were the stolen locus stones to think about, too, but those had nothing to do with me, even though the magisters thought they did.

Once I'd worked out the problems, I could get out of the ducal magister's rooms and go back to living at Heartsease, and maybe Nevery would stop worrying about me all the time.

So, the kidnappers. I'd been wondering what kind of person sent men with fists to beat people up and then grab them, somebody who knew a lot about thieving, and I had a cold, snaky feeling in my chest that was telling me who that person might be. Somebody from the Twilight who wasn't supposed to be here in Wellmet.

Crowe, maybe.

When I was a little kid, Crowe had killed my mother, who was his sister, and he'd tried to turn me into his heir, the next Underlord. Instead of letting him do that, I'd run away and hidden in the streets of the Twilight, trying to keep out of his minions' hands, because every time they caught me they beat the fluff out of me and then dragged me back to the Dusk House. Then Crowe used his clicker-ticker, a palm-sized counting device made of metal with notched bone discs, to calculate just what I'd hate most as a punishment. *Click-tick-tick* with the clicker-ticker, and that would be three days locked in a dark room with nothing to eat. Just thinking of

Crowe made a misery eel hatch and squirm around in my stomach.

There was only one way to be sure if it was him. Magic. The finding spell was big and complicated, and I couldn't do it here, not with a guard outside the door and servants all over the place, so I'd need to get out of the Dawn Palace and out of the Sunrise. My cousin Embre had as much to do with Crowe as I did—more, even—so I was sure as sure he'd let me do what I needed to do at Dusk House. The trick was getting over to the Twilight without any guards following me.

Digging through the books that Benet had brought, I found an old wizard's grimoire, one with lots of spells written in tiny, neat black letters, and looked up the remirrimer spell, which I could use to make a kind of shadow version of myself. Then I looked up the anstriker, a finding spell, which I also knew about but had never used.

I read over the spells until they stuck in my memory, then dumped everything out of a canvas knapsack that Benet had brought from Heartsease and refilled it with some magical things. I got to my feet and put the knapsack over my shoulders. "Pip!" I called.

The little dragon flew over from the windowsill and perched on top of the knapsack.

"Careful," I said. I'd put two glass scrying globes in there, and they would shatter if they got bumped too hard.

The guard was waiting outside the door. "Where are you going, Ducal Magister?" she asked, as I set off down the hallway.

I ignored the *ducal magister* part of her question. "To the library." That wasn't a lie; I really was going there first.

Rowan had once shown me the Dawn Palace library. The academicos library just had books and scrolls about magic, but the palace library had books about lots of other things, every book ever printed in Wellmet, plus other books from other cities. It took up half of the second floor of the palace, a big room with rows of tall book-stuffed shelves and long tables in the center. A good place for reading; an even better place to give a palace guard the slip.

Assuming the magics didn't do something strange when I tried the remirrimer spell, that is.

Followed by the guard, I went in the library door, past some tables where a few people were reading quietly, and toward the rows of bookshelves. At the end of the alley between two long shelves, I paused. "I have to look at a book," I said to the guard. "Will you wait here?"

She nodded and folded her arms. Very alert.

Pretending to examine the books, I walked slowly through the narrow way between the two shelves. Here, all the way at the other end, where the light was dimmest. This was a good place. I stopped and stared straight ahead at a book set on the shelf. *A Young Person's Guide to Fighting Cephalopods*, the book was called. Slowly I reached up and put my hand on Pip's claw-paw where it clung to one of the knapsack straps.

All right, you magics. Let's do this right.

Whispering, I said the remirrimer spell. When I got to the end of it, Pip gave a little shiver and coughed out a fist-sized ball of writhing light and shadow. It hung in the air right by my shoulder.

Krrrr, Pip said.

So far, so good.

I held my breath, hoping the guard wouldn't see what happened next.

As I stepped aside, the shadow expanded, taking shape and gathering substance, until a shadow-me stood beside me. It wore a knapsack and a scruffy black sweater, and had a crest of black hair shadowing its face, and it stared straight ahead at the kid-fighting-squid book on the shelf.

Then, with a *whumph*, all the doors and windows of the library flew open and then slammed closed again. At the other end of the bookshelf, the guard whirled away to look. From the other people in the library came shouts of surprise. The books shivered on their shelves.

With a rush of power, the magics poured into the shadow-me, and he started to grow. First he was just tall, and then he grew bigger and bigger until he was looming over the shaking bookshelves. He stood with his hands on his hips, grinning, his blue eyes flashing, and he really did look like me, only he was *huge* and zinging with magic. The shouts in the library turned to shrieks; the room grew dim as the shadow-me grew even larger, blocking the light. A wind leaped up and swirled around him, carrying bits of paper and dust.

"Ducal magister?" shouted the guard, her eyes wide, staring up.

It wasn't what I'd planned, but as a distraction it couldn't be any better.

I ducked from between the wobbling book-shelves and took off in the other direction; Pip clung to my shoulder. I darted around the end of the shelf and peered back to check on the guard. She had drawn her sword and was backing away from the giant shadow-me. Laughing, I skiffed across the passageway to another alley between shelves, then 'round a corner, through a room full of map books, and out into the hallway.

I heard the sound of shouting and running feet. Quick as sticks, I headed in the opposite direction.

I got away clean, out of the Dawn Palace and into the rainy city, sticking to alleys and backstreets, through the Sunrise. At the bridge I saw a pair of guards, but I hid Pip under my sweater and kept my head down, and they didn't notice me.

Finally I stepped off the bridge and onto the puddled streets of the Twilight.

Good! Now I could do the magical spell and find out who'd sent those kidnappers after me.

CHAPTER 7

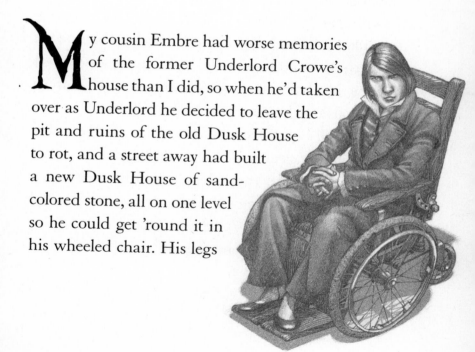

My cousin Embre had worse memories of the former Underlord Crowe's house than I did, so when he'd taken over as Underlord he decided to leave the pit and ruins of the old Dusk House to rot, and a street away had built a new Dusk House of sand-colored stone, all on one level so he could get 'round it in his wheeled chair. His legs didn't work because Crowe had had minions break them when he'd been Underlord and he'd wanted Embre out of the way, even though Embre's true name, Embre-wing, was a black bird name, and he was Crowe's own son.

I walked up to the double-wide front door. No guards were posted, but somebody was watching, because the door opened before I could knock. Pip flew up and landed on my shoulder, and a silent minion brought us down a wide, slate-paved hallway to Embre's office.

He was there, sitting in his wheeled chair beside a warm fire and small table with a tea tray set on it. Seeing me, he frowned. "A bit worse for wear, aren't you, cousin?" he asked.

"I'm all right," I said, wiping the rain off my sore face with my sleeve.

Embre's aunt, the old pyrotechnist Sparks, sat opposite him, holding a teacup in her three-fingered hand. She wore her usual gray, scorch-marked dress, and her ash-colored hair was cut short. "Whatcher, wizard boy," she said to me with a grin.

I grinned back at her. I was just as interested in pyrotechnics as she was.

"Magic's been tricksy lately," she said.

"I noticed," I said. Hmmm. As a pyrotechnist, Sparks collected slowsilver, and made blackpowder and other things that would explode if you combined them. Because they'd once been dragons, the magics loved anything that had to do with smoke or fire, and explosions like the ones Sparks did drew their attention and got them all roiled up. That would not be a very good thing for the city right now. "Sparks," I said slowly. "It'd be a good idea to not do any pyrotechnics for a while."

"Figured," Sparks agreed. "Been experimenting with tea lately, instead."

Pip dropped off my shoulder and flew across the room, landing on the arm of Sparks's chair.

"Want a sip of my blackpowder blend, do you?" Sparks said to the dragon. She held out her cup.

Pip stuck its snout into the cup and took a drink

of her new tea. It looked up at Sparks, breathed out a puff of smoke, then took another gulp.

Sparks gave a gap-toothed grin, then set her cup on the table and got to her feet. "All right then?" she said to Embre.

He nodded. "Go ahead. I'll give the ducal magister some tea if he wants it."

"Righty-o!" Sparks said, and bustled out of the room, leaving me and Embre to talk.

"*Would* the ducal magister like some tea?" Embre asked, picking up the teapot.

"I'm not the ducal magister, and I don't want any tea," I said. "I want to do some magic."

Embre raised his eyebrows. "And you had to come here to do it?"

I nodded. "Rowan and Nevery moved me into the Dawn Palace."

"I know," Embre said. "The duchess wrote me a note about it. She said you were attacked outside Heartsease. Go on. What does doing magic have to do with that?"

Right. "I was thinking about the fluff-beaters who attacked me. It could've been Crowe."

Embre's face went paper-white. "D'you think Crowe's come back?"

"I don't know," I said. "It's how he does things, though." I held up my fist.

He nodded. Crowe had been sent into exile for his crimes. But people had come back from exile before, and maybe Crowe had, too.

Embre frowned down at his hands. "I've had this feeling that something's wrong in the city," he said quietly. "Rowan's felt it, too; she mentioned it in her note. It might be because we've got two magics here and they've yet to be properly settled, but I'm not certain that's it." He looked up at me. "Maybe it's because Crowe's returned."

"Maybe," I said. "The anstriker spell will tell us if he has or not."

I pulled the small table into the middle of the room, where I put the tea tray on the floor, then took the rag-wrapped scrying globes out of my knapsack. Pip stuck its nose into the knapsack and snuffled around, its tail twitching.

Embre leaned forward in his wheeled chair so he could see what I was doing.

I unwrapped the smaller of the scrying globes. It was a glass ball about the size of a fist, but perfectly round. I gave it a polish and set it on the table. Its surface swirled with rainbow colors, so it looked like a soap bubble.

"I'm going to need some slowsilver," I said to Embre.

He nodded, and while I unwrapped the other globe, he rolled his wheeled chair to the door, opened it, and gave an order to a minion waiting outside, then wheeled back over to the table. "What do they do?" Embre asked, pointing at the fist-sized globe.

"Escry," I said. That wasn't a very good answer, so I added, "This one can see all of Wellmet." The second globe was the size of Pip, when the dragon was curled up and sleeping. I flicked it with my fingernail. It made a chiming hum. "This bigger one can see the parts of the Peninsular Duchies nearest Wellmet." If it didn't crack under the spell, which the grimoire said could happen.

Embre gave a sharp nod. "We'll be able to see if Crowe is here, then?"

I nodded. If Crowe was in Wellmet or nearby, we could be sure as sure that he'd sent those men to beat the fluff out of me and try to kidnap me, and I figured we'd know who was responsible for the locus stone thefts, too. Pushing Pip aside, I dug a set of nested metal bowls out of the knapsack and put them on the table.

The minion came in then with a glass beaker half full of slowsilver, which he set on the table. Embre sent him out again.

Carefully I set out the metal bowls and poured a bit of slowsilver in each. Then, holding them with the wormsilk cloth so I wouldn't smudge them with fingerprints, I set each scrying globe in its puddle of slowsilver. The spell could be done with water in the bowls, but using slowsilver made it stronger and gave a clearer picture, the grimoire said. That made sense—the slowsilver had once been a dragon's scales, before the dragon turned into a magical being, so the slowsilver attracted the magic's attention.

"*Tallennar*," I said, Pip's true name.

Pip popped its head out of the knapsack, then crawled up to my shoulder. I rested my hand on the dragon's back, on the smooth place between its wings. Before starting the spell, I glanced across at Embre.

"You'd better go out for this part," I said.

He raised his eyebrows. "Why, Cousin?" he asked.

Because spells didn't always work the way they were supposed to when I did them, was why, and the two-magics problem could make it even worse. "It might be dangerous," I said.

"I'll take my chances," Embre said. "Get on with it."

All right.

I moved the smaller scrying globe in its dish to the edge of the table so Embre could see. Keeping one hand on Pip, I touched the globe with the tips of my fingers and started the anstriker spell. As I spoke the spellwords, the surface of the globe swirled with rainbow colors, like oil on water. The inside of the globe darkened until it was the shadowy black of a Twilight alleyway.

Under my fingers, the globe tingled. The darkness inside it brightened slowly, revealing a view of the city, but small, a tiny version of Wellmet shaped to the curve of the glass globe. We saw the narrow, steep streets, the tumbledown houses, and the factories of the Twilight with tiny wisps of smoke coming from their chimneys. Then the river twisting through the city like a little brown snake, and then the bright Sunrise on the other side.

I glanced up at Embre. "Ready?"

He nodded. He leaned forward to see, gripping the arms of his chair.

Because Crowe was a true name, as soon as I

said it out loud, the globe would escry for him.

I took a deep breath. "*Crowe*," I whispered.

A tiny spell-spark flared up inside the globe. It started its search at the Dawn Palace and raced downhill from there, through the wide streets and stone houses and parks of the Sunrise. At a street near the river, the spark slowed down, as if sniffing out some faint scent, but then it went on, zooming over the bridge and into the Twilight, racing along the river and the mudflats, through the factories, through the Deeps and the Steeps. Embre and I leaned close, watching the streets and houses flicker past. We saw the old Dusk House pit, and then the new Dusk House. The spark flared, shadows swirled, and the inside of the globe turned black.

Embre grabbed my sleeve, his hand like a claw. "Well?"

I lifted my fingers from the globe. "The spell slowed down in the Sunrise, did you see?"

He nodded, still staring at the globe. "Does that mean he's there?"

I wasn't sure. "I don't think so," I said slowly. "The spark would've stopped and flared up if he was, and there's no way to hide from the anstriker spell." No way that I knew of, anyway.

"Good," Embre said. "Now be sure he's not coming here or lurking somewhere outside the city."

I pushed aside the smaller globe and pulled the larger globe in its bowl of slowsilver to the edge of the table. I did the thing with the anstriker spell and the true name.

This time the globe showed a dragon's-eye view of the lands around Wellmet and beyond, a long, wide stretch of ocean-edged land with tiny cities and trade roads and vast green forests and rivers that glinted like silver threads, and mountains that scraped against the inside of the glass. The spell-spark began at the dark spot that was Wellmet and circled outward, slowly at first, like a bee circling a flower. The spell-spark grew larger, and flew faster, a ball of sparks whooshing past the desert and the city of Desh, then swirling over a carpet of forest and darting among tall mountain peaks, burning more and more brightly.

For just a second Dusk House faded away and I felt the two magics overhead, shifting like two huge, impatient dragons, tied together, yet straining against each other. I strained just as hard to hold on to the spell.

It slipped away. Under my fingers, the surface of the glass globe buzzed like a thousand angry wasps. The sparks burst into flame; the flames expanded until they filled the entire globe. The glass grew warm, then sizzling hot.

I jerked my hand away from the globe and leaped back. The rainbow glass darkened to molten red and the slowsilver in the metal dish bubbled and boiled. Flames crackled on the inside curve of the globe. Then, right in its center, a new, white-bright light blossomed and expanded.

As I shouted a warning, Embre pushed his wheeled chair away from the table, covering his head. I threw myself to the floor. A sharp crack and crash, and the scrying globe exploded, shards of burning glass shooting like arrows through the air, shattering against the walls and ceiling. Sparks swarmed around the room. A thick cloud of gray-black smoke billowed up and swirled. Pip crouched on the table, blinking.

From out in the hallway came the sound of running feet, and then two minions flung open the door and rushed into the room. Their feet crunched on the shattered glass. "Underlord, are you all right?" one of them asked.

Embre had ended up across the room against the wall. He coughed and waved smoke away from his face. Blood seeped from a thin cut on his cheek. "I'm fine," he said sharply. "Thanks for coming so quickly. Go wait outside."

The minions nodded and went out.

The room fell silent. The smoke drifted up to the ceiling and hung there. Overhead, the magics settled again, but I could still feel their uneasiness. I got up from the floor.

Embre coughed again. "So," he said, after another silent moment. "He's not here."

I shook my head. Crowe wasn't in Wellmet, and he wasn't anywhere near the city, either.

Embre let out his breath and rested his head on his hand, which was shaking. He'd been a lot more worried about Crowe than I'd realized.

"You all right?" I asked, stepping closer.

"Yes." He wiped the blood off his face. "Ow."

"Sorry about that," I said.

He looked at the smear of blood on his hand, then gave me a shaky grin. "Well, Cousin, I am the Underlord, but I'm also a pyrotechnist. I've seen explosions before."

True, he had.

"And you did warn me," he said.

Yes. I had.

"I'm glad Crowe's not here," he added.

A shudder of dread crept up my back, thinking of Crowe. "So am I."

CHAPTER 8

After collecting as much of the slowsilver as I could coax back into a glass beaker and then wrapping the scrying globe in its wormsilk cloth, I said good-bye to Embre and left.

At the front door of Dusk House, Sparks was waiting for me.

Pip, seeing her, twitched its tail. "No more blackpowder tea for you, Pip," I said.

Sparks grinned at me and Pip; then she edged closer. "Got a bit of information you might like to know, eh?"

Information? "What?" I asked.

"One of them magister wizards has been asking 'round the Twilight for pyrotechnic materials."

That was strange. The magisters hated pyrotechnics; once they'd banished me from the city and almost hanged me as punishment for doing pyrotechnic spells. And now that we had two magics in the city, the risks of setting off explosions were even bigger. "Who was it?"

"Dunno what his name was. Scrawny." Sparks pointed at her head. "Big ears."

Magister Nimble, it sounded like. That didn't make sense at all; Nimble hated me, and pyrotechnics, more than any of the other magisters. *And* he'd had his locus stone stolen, he'd said. Strange. But there wasn't anything I could do about it now. "If you hear anything else, tell me, all right?"

"Righty-o!" Sparks said, grinning.

I said good-bye to her and stepped out the front

door of Dusk House and stopped. We'd spent the afternoon on the anstriker spell, and now it was night.

Oh, no. Rowan was expecting me for dinner.

The streets were dark and empty, and my hurrying footsteps sounded loud on the wet cobblestones. Pip dropped off my shoulder and flew ahead, pausing to perch on shop signs and on piles of trash in the street, then flying ahead again. As I turned a corner onto a street that would lead me to the Night Bridge, I caught a glimpse, out of the corner of my eye, of shadowy figures. Following me.

My heart jolted with fright. The kidnappers! I looked around for Pip. *"Tallennar!"* I whispered. A rustle of wings and Pip was there, scrambling up my leg and onto my shoulder, where it crouched, lashing its tail. I stared into the street behind me.

Two dark shapes loomed up. I flinched back and got ready to run and shout my new dazzler spell at the same time.

"No harm, Blackbird," one of the shapes said, a deep, gravelly voice.

I let out my breath. Not the men who'd beaten the fluff out of me, then. Fist. One of Embre's men. And beside him, his partner, Hand.

"What d'you want?" I asked.

"Nothing," Fist said. Beside him, Hand nodded.

"What're you doing, then?" I asked.

"Underlord told us to keep an eye on you, little bird," Fist said. "When you're in the Twilight. You see the men what did that"—he pointed at my face—"and you give us the nod, right? We want a word with 'em." He held up his fist to show what kind of word it would be.

Embre had sent his men to watch me? To protect me when I was in the Twilight?

Curse it. More fuss and worry. More *looking after.*

With Pip clinging to my coat with its claws, I stepped off the Night Bridge and into the Sunrise part of the city. Captain Kerrn was there. Scowling, she stepped in front of me. Behind her, the wide street, lit by werelights, led up the hill. Kerrn reached out to grab me by the front of the sweater so she could slam me against a wall and growl at me, but then she jerked her hand back and rested it on her sword pommel.

"Where have you been?" She bit off her words and spat them out. Angry.

I shrugged. I was coming off the bridge; clear as clear I'd been in the Twilight.

When she saw I wasn't going to answer, she whirled and started stalking up the street. "You have missed dinner with the duchess. And another locus magicalicus has been stolen."

Oh, no. Not another one. I'd lost my locus stone once; I knew what a horrible, empty, desperate thing that was. I hurried a little to catch up with her. "Whose stone?"

"One belonging to another magister. Sandera. Taken from her workroom."

Big trouble, then. Kerrn probably thought that's what I'd been off doing during the afternoon, stealing Sandera's locus stone.

We headed up the street, passing the tall stone houses and shops and the werelights, which cast pink light across the stone pavements.

"Tell me what is going on," Kerrn said suddenly. "You can trust me."

I blinked. I trusted her to toss me into a prison cell if she thought I belonged there. "I didn't steal the locus stones, Kerrn," I said.

"No," she said. "I do not mean the thefts. You were attacked. You are in trouble of some kind. Your safety has been entrusted to me. You must tell me what is going on."

"I don't know what's going on," I said. She wouldn't believe that, sure as sure. Maybe I could drink truth-telling phlister and tell her and *then* she'd believe me.

She stopped and pointed at my bruised face. "I will not allow you to be hurt again."

Wait. She was worried about me getting the fluff beaten out of myself? "I'm being careful," I said.

"*Careful?* Is that what you call it?" She leaned closer. "I will make sure you are more careful." She glared down at me, then whirled and headed up the street.

So Kerrn was looking after me, too. Drats.

As we came into the Dawn Palace, there were more guards than usual at the front doors, and Kerrn had a couple of quick, brisk words with them. Then she "accompanied" me to the ducal magister's rooms and left me there with two guards at the door. Pip prowled the shadowy edges of the room, its tail twitching, then came over and nosed at the window. I opened it and the dragon flew out. It didn't like the Dawn Palace, either. And it probably wanted to hunt for pigeons. After closing the window, I shoved aside a couple of fringed, lumpy-laced pillows and sat on the window seat and looked out at the night. What I really needed to do was go out again so I could walk through the city and sense what was going on with the magics. But I was tired and I wouldn't get past Kerrn's guards, not tonight.

There was a knock on the door. Go away, who-ever you are.

The door opened. Rowan.

She said something to the guard outside and came in.

Just inside the door, she stopped and looked around at the ducal magister's room, frowning. "This is not what I was expecting." She shook her head. "Curse it."

Then she went to one of the tall wooden chairs beside the hearth, shoved it around so it faced the window seat where I was sitting, and sat down. She wrinkled her nose. "Connwaer, you smell like smoke."

I raised my arm and sniffed at my sweater-sleeve. I did smell like smoke. From the anstriker spell gone wrong. She didn't want to hear about that, though. "I was doing some magic," I said.

She raised her eyebrows.

"I am a wizard," I reminded her.

"Mmm. It's cold in here," she said, rubbing her arms. "The servants should have built a fire."

They should have, but they wouldn't come into my rooms. They were afraid of Pip, I guessed. My stomach gave an empty growl.

"You didn't get anything to eat, did you?" Rowan said. "I'll send the servants with dinner."

I could definitely eat dinner. Maybe they'd bring hot biscuits and chicken pie like Benet baked. "Thanks," I said.

She smiled. "You're very welcome." Her smile faded. "I'm very sorry about the rooms. I know you don't like them. I told Miss Dimity to be sure they would be warm and comfortable for you, but she misunderstood. I should have seen to it myself."

"You didn't have time," I muttered.

"That's right." She sighed. "I know this is hard for you, Conn, but you'll get used to it here, and you'll find that being the ducal magister isn't so bad if you just give it a chance."

It didn't matter if I gave it a chance, and it didn't matter if Rowan made the ducal magister's rooms more comfortable. I didn't belong here. Suddenly I felt a wave of homesickness for Nevery and Benet and the cozy study at Heartsease. I curled up and put my arms around my knees.

Rowan sighed again and rubbed her eyes. She looked tired. "At dinner we talked about the theft of the locus magicalicus stones," she said at last.

I was glad I'd missed that, anyway.

"Neither one of them has turned up yet, as Keeston's stolen stone did. As you can imagine, the magisters are in an uproar."

"They're good at uproar," I said.

"Yes, I suppose they are." Rowan got up from the uncomfortable chair and sat down on the window seat next to me. She looked beautiful in her green dress, with her hair braided and pinned up on top of her head. "Conn, they're pushing me very hard to arrest you for this latest theft. Where have you been all afternoon? What magic were you doing? Why did you miss dinner?"

I scowled at her. "Ro, I don't need all this *looking after.*"

"I'm not so sure about that, my lad," she said. "I'm worried. There's something strange going on. Not only the locus stone thefts. It's a feeling, as if there's a . . ." She shook her head. "I don't know. Something wrong. Maybe that doesn't make any sense."

I stayed quiet. I had thieves and kidnappers to deal with, and the two-magics problem; I couldn't do anything about this other *something wrong*.

"I'm not the only one who feels it. Kerrn has the guard on high alert. She's on edge about it."

If Kerrn had any more edge, she'd cut herself.

Rowan gave a brisk nod. "With all of that, and those attackers on the loose, and the magisters insisting that you be arrested for thievery, it really is a good thing you're living here under my protection, instead of at Heartsease. You'll be safer as long as you stay in the Dawn Palace."

By *safer* she meant Kerrn and her guards following me around all the time. "But Ro, there's things I have to do."

"You have to be more careful," she said.

"I *am* careful."

She gave me an exasperated look. "Conn, today you tricked your guard and went into the Twilight alone, where you apparently did a magical spell that left you smelling like smoke. You are *not* careful." She folded her arms. "You are the ducal magister now. You simply must learn to act like it."

There she was, shoving me into the ducal magister box again. "Ro, I never agreed to that," I reminded her.

She stood up. "All right. Fine. Any moment now Miss Dimity is going to pop in here to remind me that I'd better go to bed because I have an early meeting in the morning. So good night, Connwaer." She headed for the door, then paused and pulled a heavy-looking bag out of her pocket and tossed it on the table. It made a jingling sound when it landed. "Oh, and here," she said crossly. "It's your pay for serving as ducal magister."

Then she left, slamming the door behind her.

CHAPTER 9

I didn't want any pay for being the ducal magister. Still, I went over to investigate the bag. It was full of money—silver locks and even some golden sun coins. More money than I knew what to do with. I hid it away on a shelf behind some books

and went to the door to have a look at the lock.

I was just about to bring out my lockpick wires to see if I could open and close it—just to keep myself sharp—when the door was flung open, knocking me over, and Miss Dimity stepped into the room.

I scrambled to my feet, shoving the wires back into my pocket.

"The dragon is not here with the ducal magister," she announced to the green-liveried servants behind her. "It is safe to enter."

Some of the servants brought coal and started a fire; she waved the rest to a table near the hearth. After eyeing the deep scratches on the back of the chair Pip liked to perch on, she gave me one of her scraped-on smiles.

"Ducal Magister," she said, with a stiff bow. "Your dinner." She handed me a napkin and pointed at the Pip-scratched chair.

I sat in it. My stomach rumbled.

Servants trooped in and, casting cautious-curious looks at me, laid out plates and forks, and covered dishes, enough to crowd three of the little tables.

Miss Dimity swept the cover off the first dish. Something gray and wobbly. "Jellied eel with horse-radish sauce," she proclaimed. Another dish with a lump of bluish-white stuff in it: "Eggplant surprise!" A bowl: "Cabbage soup." Another plate: "Piebald beans." And last: "With candied fern-frond for dessert." She pointed to a teapot. "Tea." She nodded as a servant added a last plate covered with a white napkin. "And, as ordered especially for you by the duchess, biscuits."

She stepped back and waited as all the other servants went out; then she left, closing the door behind her with a polite *click*.

I looked over the food. I'd start with the biscuits, of course, though I knew they wouldn't be as good as Benet's biscuits, hot out of the oven and dripping with butter and honey.

These biscuits were a brownish-gray color and were arranged on a plate around a little pot of greasy-looking butter and a sprig of some sort of greenery. I tried one. Hard and tasting a bit like ash. Even the biscuits I baked were better than this!

The cabbage soup sounded like the best of the rest of it, but when I tried a bite, it was cold. None of the other food was hot, either; it was all cold as cobblestones, and so was the tea. The kitchens were far away from the ducal magister's rooms, I guessed. I dunked one of the ashy biscuits in the soup, which tasted like salted washwater, and ate a few bites, but didn't feel like eating any more.

In the hearth, the fire roared. The servants had lit fires in the other rooms, too, because Rowan had ordered them to make it more cozy in here, but now it was getting stuffy and hot. The bedroom was hottest of all, so I took the blankets off the bed and slept on the floor in the main room with the windows wide open.

In the morning I woke up with the fire dead in the grate, frosty air pouring in the windows, and

Pip crouched on my chest, glaring at me with its ember-red eyes.

"Hello, you," I said, and my voice sounded rusty.

Pip opened its maw and dropped something onto my chest. I picked it up and used the edge of the blanket to wipe the dragon spit off it. Pushing Pip off me, sitting up in my blankets, I examined it. A stone. It fizzed in my hand, making my fingers tingle. It was deep purple, round, and rough, about the size of a quail's egg. A locus magicalicus. Sandera's stolen stone, sure as sure. I got to my feet and looked down at Pip, crouched on the floor next to me. "Where'd you get this?" I asked.

Krrrr, Pip said. It crawled onto my abandoned blankets, wrapping its tail around itself.

Busy night, clear as clear.

I crouched down next to the nest of blankets. "You didn't steal it, did you Pip?"

The little dragon blinked, then closed its eyes.

Had Pip stolen Sandera's stone? Maybe. More likely, the dragon had stolen the locus stone back from the thieves, whoever they were. Why else would Pip be bringing the stones to me? If it wanted the stones for itself, it'd just swallow them, as it had swallowed mine.

Getting to my feet, I set the locus stone on the table. Then I washed and found some clean clothes and got dressed.

I was pulling my black sweater on over my head when a knock came at the door, and a piece of paper, folded, slid under it. As I went to pick it up, I heard footsteps hurrying away, a servant too frightened to wait for me to open the door.

A note from Nevery.

Connwaer. The magisters have called a meeting for this morning to discuss the thefts of locus magicalicus stones. You must attend. DO NOT BE LATE.

— Nevery

The last thing I wanted to do this morning was go to a meeting where I'd be shouted at by the magisters. Especially with Sandera's stolen stone on me. Still, if Nevery wanted me there, I had to go.

Not on an empty stomach, though. Because I had a ferocious dragon with me, the servants wouldn't bring breakfast to my room unless they had a direct order from Rowan, so I settled sleeping Pip on my shoulder, slipped Sandera's stone into my pocket, and went looking for food.

When I stepped out of my rooms, two guards were at the door. They both followed me while I found the kitchens. The cook shooed me and Pip out, but told me to wait in the hallway while she found me something to eat.

"Nothing fancy," I called after her, as she went back inside.

She came out with a plate of hot rolls and butter and jam. "You're that wizard boy, aren't you?"

I had a dragon riding on my shoulder; who else would I be? I nodded.

The cook looked me up and down, hands on hips. "You are too thin. You should eat more. And what about that?" She pointed at Pip. "Does this . . . animal need anything?"

I grinned at her, and she backed away a step. "No," I said. Not unless she had some pigeons flying around in the kitchen. I took two of the hot rolls from the plate and ate a big bite. Mmmm. "Thanks," I said to the cook, who nodded and went back into the kitchen. I held a roll out to the guards. "Want some?" I asked.

They didn't eat while on duty, they said.

Munching on breakfast, with Pip still asleep on my shoulder, its snout nestled against my neck, I headed out of the Dawn Palace. At the front gate, standing on the gravelly drive, I stopped and looked back.

"Ah, sir?" one of the guards asked.

I ignored him. The Dawn Palace. A fancy prison. Rowan wanted me to give it a chance, and I'd done that. I wasn't coming back to live in those too-hot, too-cold ducal magister's rooms, with the nasty fancy food, and closets full of silk-stiff clothes, and guards outside every door, and Miss Dimity bulging her eyes at me. If Nevery wouldn't let me come back to Heartsease, well, I'd figure something else out.

That decided, I headed down the hill. The guards followed. The air was chilly, the streets bustling with people and carriages and hansom cabs.

When they saw I was heading for the bridge, one of the guards cleared his throat. "Sir?"

Him calling me *sir* was about the stupidest thing I'd ever heard. I ignored him and swallowed down the last bite of buttered-and-jammed roll.

"Ducal Magister Connwaer?" he said.

I stopped. "What."

One of the guards stayed behind me; the other stepped in front, blocking my way. People passing us on the street stared as they walked by. It probably looked to them like I was being arrested. The guard said, "Magister, we're supposed to report with you to Captain Kerrn if you attempt to go into the Twilight."

It really was starting to sound like I was a prisoner. I glared at the guard. "I'm not going to the Twilight. I'm going to a meeting at Magisters Hall."

"That's all right, then," said the guard behind me.

They let me go on, following me across the bridge and down the steps to the tunnel that led under the river to the wizards' islands. We came to one of the tunnel gates. I plucked sleeping Pip off my shoulder and held it up to the gate's magic lock and said the opening spell. Pip twitched and blinked, giving me a surly look, and then touched the lock with its snout. The lock clicked open. We went through the gate, then two more gates, then through the Magisters Hall gate and up the stairs to the building itself.

At the top of the stairs was a long, stone hallway, and it was filled with wizards and apprentices and magisters in their fine robes, all talking in little groups, waiting for the meeting to begin. When they saw me with the two guards looming up behind me and Pip on my shoulder, they stared, whispering. *Stolen*, I heard, and *thief.*

Annoyed, Pip lashed its tail and snorted out a puff of gray smoke. I put my hand into my pocket to be sure Sandera's stone was still there.

I heard footsteps on the stairs behind me—*step step tap*—and then Nevery was beside me, leaning on his cane. "Good morning, Connwaer," he said mildly.

I was annoyed, too. "Not really, Nevery," I said, and I wanted to ask him if he was missing me, but he didn't seem to be, so I kept quiet.

He snorted. "The morning is not going to get any better, either." He started down the hallway. "Yet another locus magicalicus stone went missing during the night. Brumbee's. Come along. It's time to start the meeting."

The other magisters headed for the meeting room, too, Brumbee in his bright yellow robe looking rumpled and worried, and sharp Trammel who ran the medicos, and Periwinkle with her gray hair in its usual messy bun, and bat-faced Nimble. Coming last was sharp, clever Sandera. They muttered to one another while we went into the meeting room, me shedding my guards at the door.

Here was my chance. Once I'd picked Nevery's locus stone from his cloak pocket. Sure as sure I could do a reverse pocket-pick. On feather feet, I hovered behind Sandera. As she stopped beside her chair, I pulled her locus stone from my pocket and—*quick hands*—dropped it into the pocket of her magister's robe. She sat down, not noticing a thing, and I went on, finding a seat about halfway down the table and slouching into it, my hands in my pockets. Pip hopped up to perch on the back of my chair. My heart pounded a little. I watched Sandera out of the corner of my eye, but she still hadn't noticed anything.

Nevery was the leader of the magisters, so he sat at the head of the long table and, when everyone was sitting, started the meeting.

"Well, Brumbee," Nevery said. "Report."

"Oh, dear," Brumbee said. He clasped and unclasped his plump hands, which were shaking, and looked around the table. "As you all know, another locus stone has been, ah, stolen. This time it was my own. And I hear no call from it at all. Nothing. It has simply disappeared."

I frowned. That was strange. Even if his stone was gone, Brumbee should be able to feel where it was.

"What happened?" Trammel asked sharply.

Brumbee cast him an unhappy look. "*Nothing* happened. I was being careful, of course. The door to my bedroom was locked. No one could have gotten in. But I woke up this morning and my locus magicalicus was gone from the table beside my bed. Stolen."

"Impossible," Periwinkle said, shaking her head. "The stone would have killed the thief."

Nimble leaned forward. "And my own locus

stone as well—simply gone! And Sandera's, as well."

Sandera looked up, and then cocked her head, as if she was listening to something. I knew what it was—she'd just picked up the call of her locus magicalicus. In not too long she'd find it in her pocket.

Nimble caught my eye and gave a secret smirk-look, as if he knew something that I didn't. "My fellow magisters," he went on, "we do know one thief who has shown that he can handle another wizard's locus magicalicus."

Me, he meant.

"Oh, no," Brumbee said. "We can't possibly think—" He glanced at me. "He wouldn't—"

"Yes he would," Nimble said in his whiny voice. "He held the apprentice Keeston's stone the other day when his little pet brought it to him. And he once stole Nevery's locus stone, didn't he? Picked it right from his pocket!" He stood up and pointed at me while pointing his smirk at Nevery. "Well, Nevery? Didn't he?"

Nevery, scowling, opened his mouth to answer,

when Nimble went on. "And his first locus magicalicus was a jewel stolen from the ducal regalia! Who else could it be if not him and his dragon?"

I sat up straighter in my chair. "It wasn't me," I said. And not Pip, either.

"Prove it!" Trammel shouted, jumping to his feet.

"He's well known to be a liar and a thief," Nimble said. "We should have hanged him when we had the chance!"

Scowling, Nevery started to answer back, and Brumbee pulled at Trammel's sleeve, saying, "Do sit down, Trammel. Do."

From the back of my chair, Pip made a low growling sound, then it leaped into the air and flew to one of the room's narrow windows. It wanted out.

So did I.

Trying to ignore the shouts zinging from one end of the table to the other, I pushed back my chair and went to the window. Pip perched on the sill, which was about chest-high to me. I unlatched the window and pushed it open. Pip launched itself into the chilly air, flapping across the narrow courtyard that lay before Magisters Hall.

I glanced over my shoulder. Nevery stood leaning on the table, glowering at the other magisters. Brumbee sat beside him looking worried, and the rest of them were red-faced and angry, too.

Trammel stood at his place, smoke coming out of his ears. Beside him, Nimble smirked. He jabbed his finger toward me. "There's your thief!"

Thief. It was always like this. They weren't going to believe me no matter what I said.

Still . . . I knew how thieves worked. If I could get away from all the fuss and *looking after* and the ducal magister box that I didn't fit into, I could get out into the city, and once I was in the city I could sneak and spy and find out who was really stealing the locus magicalicus stones, and deal with the two-magic problem too, if I could find time for it.

"We must call the guard and have him arrested!" Trammel shouted.

I turned back to the window. The meeting room was on the ground floor of Magisters Hall. Quick as sticks, I pulled myself up and crouched on the windowsill. I pushed the window wider open.

"Connwaer—" I heard Nevery's warning shout.

A quick glance back at him—*sorry, Nevery*—and I turned and gripped the window frame, swung myself down, and dropped. Farther than it looked; I spilled onto the hard stone of the courtyard. Scrambling to my feet, I started to run. From the window behind me I heard shouts.

Near the front steps of the Magisters Hall was an entrance to the tunnels. I raced for it. "Pip!" I called. The dragon was nowhere to be seen. I reached the top of the stairs leading down to the tunnel; behind me, the front doors of the Hall burst open. The guards!

"Tallennar!" I shouted Pip's true name, and pelted down into the tunnel, my boots pounding on the stone steps. I heard the guards shout, coming after me.

I reached the Magisters Hall gate. Closed. I whirled and saw the guards' dark shadows at the very top of the stairs. Come *on*, Pip! I couldn't open the gate without my locus stone!

With a flash, Pip shot past the charging guards, through the tunnel, and slammed into my chest. I turned and shoved the dragon up against the lock and shouted out the opening spell.

The gate crashed open. As the guards reached the bottom of the stairs and lunged after me, I leaped through, and the gate slammed closed behind me. I jerked away from it before the guards could grab me with their long arms.

One guard pounded at the gate, then shook at the bars. "Come back here!" the other shouted.

Not likely. Still clutching Pip, I turned and skiffed away.

Free!

CHAPTER 10

It takes a while to work up a good layer of grime. When I'd been a little kid living on the streets of the Twilight, I'd been grimy all the time. My hair had been stiff with dirt and grease, my face smudged with dirt, my hands and feet grained with dirt and under my fingernails black with it, my tattery clothes, layers of them in the cold months, stained and smelly.

If I was going to do what I needed to do, I needed to grime

up again. Staying in the alleyways, I headed deeper into the Twilight, keeping an eye open for old rags and clothes in the piles of trash I passed. Not too far from Sark Square, I stopped in at a swagshop, trading my good stout boots and red knitted socks for a broken-down pair of shoes and a handful of copper locks. Too bad about the boots, really. But a good pair of boots would be a dead giveaway.

Carrying the bundle of rags I picked up along the way, and the old shoes, I headed for the worst part of the Twilight, the Rat Hole. Embre had been working to improve things in the Underlord's part of the city, but he hadn't changed much here, at least not yet.

I could still feel the comforting presence of the magics, though—the stony strength of Arhionvar and the warmer old Wellmet magic. Even though I was alone, I wasn't really alone.

The streets grew narrower and clotted with mud and trash, the houses on either side boarded up or burned out, leaning against one another like old men drunk on redstreak gin. I made a couple of turns to be sure nobody was following, then edged down a dead-end alley. I sat down with my back against a rotting wooden wall to see what I'd come up with.

A man's shirt with the collar and cuffs ripped off and suspicious-looking rusty-red stains down the front, and a slit over the heart where a knife might've gone in. Another shirt, yellowed, dirty wool, more moth-eaten hole than cloth. A sock with holes in the toe and heel. What had once been a gentleman's waistcoat but was now a tattered vest stiff with dirt.

Well, all right. Better than any fancy-fine ducal magister clothes, anyway.

Along with the copper lock coins I'd gotten from the swagshop lady, I had a little knife in my pocket, a silver one good for picking easy locks. I pulled it out and used it to hack off the ends of my trousers, then pulled at the dangling threads to make them look more raggedy. I had a couple of lockpick wires in the seams of my trousers; I left them there. Picking up a clot of mud, I rubbed it over my bare feet and legs, and then I put on the one sock, then the shoes. They both had holes in the soles, so I'd feel the cold cobbles under my feet. Not such a bad thing, the holes. They'd remind me of where I was and what I was.

Next, the shirts. I stood up and pulled off my black woolen sweater. I set it aside, then stripped off my good shirt and pulled on the other two ragged shirts and the dirty vest. Then I scooped up more dirt from the ground and rubbed it all over my hands and the back of my neck, and up into my hair, and smudged it across my face, too.

Finished, I looked at myself. Gutterboy.

It was a strange, free feeling, being a gutterboy again. It meant I could do whatever I wanted to do, without anybody telling me where I had to live, and no bothersome *looking after.*

I glanced down, seeing the black sweater where I'd left it folded on the ground. Drats. Benet had knitted that sweater for me; I couldn't just leave it in the alleyway. I took a shaky breath and steadied myself. No, I was free of all that and I had something to do, and I was going to do it.

"What about you, Pip?" I said.

The little dragon was perched on a broken-down box. I crouched, and it gave me a glary look with its ember eye.

"I can't have a dragon following me around," I said to it. People would notice that, sure as sure, and what I needed was to be not noticed.

Hmmm. With the magics so unsettled, this could be tricky. But something like the embero spell and the remirrimer might work. I closed my eyes and thought it through, putting the words of the other two spells together to make a new spell. The embirrimer spell. Very useful. Good for making a disguise for locus magicalicus dragons.

I opened my eyes, ready.

Perched on the box, Pip eyed me, half opening its wings as if it might fly away. Reaching out, I laid my hand on the smooth place between the dragon's golden wings and spoke the new spell.

At first nothing happened—maybe the magics were so unsettled they couldn't hear me. I frowned and tried again. This time the spell effected. Slowly at first. Pip's eyes popped wide open; then it leaped up, did a flip in the air, and, in a shower of sparks, landed on the muddy ground. White-bright light flashed.

I flinched back, covering my eyes, and blinked the brights away to see. Then I laughed. Pip crouched on the dirt in front of me, its tail lashing, its ears laid back, its whiskers twitching. A cat. But with goldy-green fur and ember-red eyes.

"Come here, you," I said, and made a grab for the Pip-cat. It yowled and scrambled away, then made an awkward leap into the air. Landing on its four paws again, it growled, then leaped again. Trying to fly.

"No wings," I said.

Pip-cat paced in a tight circle, then snarled at me and bounded out of the alley.

"Sorry, Pip!" I shouted after it.

But I wasn't, really. Being changed into a cat wasn't such a bad thing.

The last thing I did was use a copper lock to buy a stub of pencil and a bit of paper from a rag-and-bone shop, and wrote a note.

Nevery,

I'm going to find out who's been stealing the locus stones. Tell Rowan and Embre not to send guards or minions or anybody to look for me, because I need to sneak and spy and people looking for me will just get me into trouble.

Don't send Benet after me either.

If I find out anything important, I'll come to Heartsease and tell you.

—Conn

Then, after thinking for a minute, I added another line at the end.

Nevery, I think you're right that something's going on. It's not just the locus stones, it's something else.

·⊙̣ ⊙̈   ⋔⊙̂⌒⌒⊙̈⌒⊙̣⌒8⋀:
⊥̂

From the Duchess Rowan to Underlord Embre

I suppose you've heard from Magister Nevery that Conn has run away from a meeting at Magisters Hall. I am furious with him, of course, because it makes the magisters more certain that he's the thief responsible for the locus stone thefts. I think we ought to be searching the city for Conn. It isn't safe for him out there. The palace guards, led by Captain Kerrn, could search the Sunrise and your men can search the Twilight.

Duchess Rowan Forestal
Dawn Palace
The Sunrise

Dear Rowan,

Yes, I heard about Conn's disappearance. My people are staying alert, though not searching. I should warn you that we might not have any luck. Conn hid from Crowe for years. He knows all the back alleyways and dark corners of the Twilight and will not be easy to track—assuming he's here, of course, and not hiding somewhere in the Sunrise. Anyway, I think we made a mistake, before. I had people watching him, you had guards following him. We crowded him too much, and that's why he's run away. You must remember, Ro, that you can name him the ducal magister, but my cousin is still part gutterboy.

Rowan, you're right that there is something else going on. Lately I've felt that something was wrong in my part of the city. During the past few days, it's grown to be more than a feeling. There is a kind of secret gang at work here. Men who set fires, and sabotage the machines at the factories, and break into shops, not to steal anything, just to destroy. They strike at random and then disappear. My people have tried to track them, but have had no luck. Has anything like this been happening in the Sunrise?

Yours,

Embre

Dusk House

—From Duchess to Underlord—

Curse it, Embre, we have to find him.

And yes, this invisible gang, as you're calling it, has been at work in the Sunrise, as well. The palace guards and Captain Kerrn are on high alert.

In haste,

Rowan, Duchess, etc.

Predictably, magisters see boy running away as admission of guilt. Led by Nimble, they are howling for Duchess and Captain Kerrn to have guards comb city for him, lock him up.

⌐ᴵᴏ̈ᴏᴏᴏ̂⌐ᴏ̈ ᴏᴏᴏ̈ ᴏᴏᴏ̂ᴏ̈ᴏᴏ
ᴏ̈ᴏ̈ ᴏᴏᴵ ᴏᴵᴏ̈ ᴏᴏᴏ̂ᴏᴏ
ᴏ̈ᴏ̈ᴡ: ᴏᴏᴏᴏᴏ ᴏᴏ̈ᴏ ᴏᴏ̂ᴀ
ᴏᴏᴵ ᴏᴏ ᴵᴏᴏᴏᴏᴏᴏ̈ᴏ ᴏᴵ
ᴏᴏ̂ᴏᴏᴵ:

    This morning, Benet brought up note, neatly folded black sweater, said they'd been left on Heartsease doorstep overnight. Boy wants me to tell Duchess and Underlord not to search for him. Tempted not to; rather, would do anstriker spell, then send Benet to drag him back home. Back to Dawn Palace, should say. Conn is good at hiding, though, especially if in Twilight. Searchers might cause more trouble for him, as he says. Curse it.

Also, problem of missing locus stones very serious, possibly more serious than we have yet given thought to. Sandera's stone was recovered—that is something. But Brumbee and Nimble—their stones are missing and they hear no call from them. Means the stones have immediately been taken out of the city, or their call has been silenced, somehow. Why are stones being stolen? Are they being destroyed, or used for some other purpose? Is this some kind of attack on the wizards of the city? Have decided, reluctantly, that we must leave Conn to discover this, if he can. Meanwhile, the remaining magisters—myself, Trammel, Sandera, and Periwinkle—are taking special precautions to protect our locus stones.

Meanwhile, magics becoming more problematic. Trammel reports that he has stopped using magical spells to help his patients at the medicos. Brumbee reports that the apprentices at the academicos have been instructed to stop using them as well—practice spells keep effecting in unpredictable ways.

Am beginning to think all of these threads are connected—the thievery of locus stones, the attack on Conn, the unsettled magics, and the sabotage that both the Underlord and Duchess Rowan are reporting in their parts of the city. Have dire feeling things about to get worse. Very worried.

CHAPTER
11

After three days in the back alleys of the Twilight, I was grimy enough and hungry enough, and thinking street thoughts. I'd also noticed something. The people in the Twilight were nervous. There was a lot of lurking in doorways, watchful eyes, over-the-shoulder glancing. Something was going on—or it was about to happen—and the Twilight people were wary. Me, I kept an eye out for the kidnappers, but figured they were looking for the ducal magister, not for some grubby gutterboy.

I missed Nevery and Benet and the warm kitchen at Heartsease, and I missed having shelves of books to read and biscuits to eat. But I liked going where I wanted without being worried about, too. Anyway, I couldn't go back until I found the locus stone thieves. They were around somewhere, sure as sure.

When I'd been a gutterboy, I hadn't ever talked to the other gutterboys and guttergirls who lived on the streets of the Twilight. Half of them had been working for Crowe, the Underlord, and he'd had a word out on me, and they would've turned me in to him for a copper lock and a sausage in a biscuit.

But nobody knew better than gutterboys and guttergirls what was going on in the city. We saw everything and heard everything, and nobody noticed us coming and going. I just had to find some gutterkids who would tell me what they'd seen and heard about the locus stone thefts.

And I had to do it soon. The day before, as I'd

crept through an alley, one of the black-and-white birds from the tree in front of Heartsease had spiraled down to land on a broken cobblestone at my feet. Tied to its leg was a quill, and in the quill was a note from Nevery, just a short one.

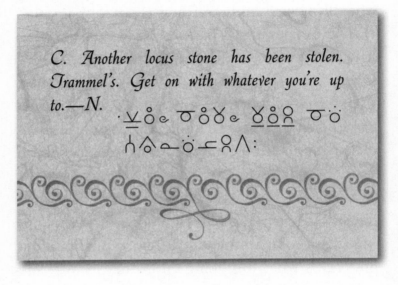

C. Another locus stone has been stolen. Trammel's. Get on with whatever you're up to.—N.

Every gutterkid knew that a good way to make a copper lock or two was to go mudlarking down by the river. In the mudflats you could find things washed up, like old clothes or shoes with some wear left in them, or a drowned man with a string of copper locks in his pocket.

Pip was still annoyed with me for turning it into a green-furred, red-eyed cat. It followed me, staying hidden, but I knew it was nearby. I really needed to settle the magics properly, but without Pip I couldn't do it. The magics would be all right for another few days, anyway.

With Pip following, I headed past the docks and warehouses, out to the edge of the city where the magics felt thin. The river curved here, and in the curve were the mudflats, a flat brown stretch dotted with clumps of river grass. Flocks of gulls circled overhead, and the air stank of mud and dead fish and open drains. A chilly wind blew off the river and the gray clouds overhead spat out an icy drizzle.

Hunching my shoulders against the wind, I followed a rutted path around the curve of the river at the edge of the mud to a windowless shack built of rotting boards with tar paper nailed up on its roof to keep the rain out. A smudge of smoke drifted from a stovepipe that stuck out of the roof. Somebody was inside, then. As I came up the path to the shack, its door creaked open and a girl stepped out.

She wore a ragged woolen dress too long for her and a holey striped shawl, and her bare feet were crusted with mud. Her long brown hair was tied back in a tail.

"What d'you want?" she asked, scowling.

I nodded at the shack. "Can I come in?"

She shook her head and pointed at the path I'd come up. "Take yourself off." Then she whirled, stepped inside, and slammed the door behind her.

Drats. I didn't have time for this. But I couldn't force my way in. Sure as sure more kids were inside, and they'd fight me if I tried it. I sat down on the path to wait.

The rain kept up. Pip stayed crouched behind its clump of grass. I shivered as a drop of cold rain wormed down my neck and inside my shirt. The kids in the shack knew I was there. They'd have to open the door sometime. I kept waiting, looking out across the mudflats and at the Night Bridge.

That was the thing about being a gutterboy. It wasn't all freedom. A lot of the time it was a hard life, and a lonely one, and it was also boring. When I'd been a gutterboy, I hadn't thought about much except food and finding a warm place to sleep, and staying out of Crowe's hands. I hadn't even known how to read.

After a long time, just as the sky was growing dark and the werelights of the Sunrise were flickering on across the river, the door creaked open again.

The girl stepped out, and this time a bigger boy came with her. He looked like a minion-in-training, with a low forehead and just one eyebrow, and narrow, suspicious eyes. He wore rags, but over the top of them he wore a man's frock coat, too big for him, but warm. He was the boss, then.

I got stiffly to my feet.

Boy-minion's narrow eyes narrowed even more, peering at me through the dim light. "Got anything to eat?"

I nodded. I'd come prepared.

He muttered something to the girl. She said something back. They both turned and went into the shack, leaving the door open behind them.

Right, I was in.

Three other kids were inside the shack, besides minion-boy and the girl, a couple of them wrapped in ragged blankets, all of them sitting on the floor around a pile of stuff washed up from the river. The air inside was warm with drafts of cold slithering through it, and it smelled like dirty socks and dried river mud. Old rope was strung across the room, right below the roof, where rags and holey clothes had been hung up to dry. The orange glow of firelight came from a battered tin stove that crouched against one wall, and shadows lurked in the corners. The mudlark-kids watched me come in, their eyes bright in their dirty faces.

I sat on the dirt floor by the door, farthest away from the warmth of the stove.

The girl put the wood she'd brought in on the

fire, and she and the boy sat down next to the stove and pretended to ignore me. The other kids peeked quick glances at me, then went back to what they were doing, which was sorting through the piles of trash they'd mudlarked. They'd sell the cloth to a rag-and-bone man, and other bits to junk sellers or swagshop owners. Had any of them ever been to school? Probably not. None of them knew how to write or read or think about much but mudlarking.

I pulled my knees up and rested my head on my folded arms. They'd get around to me eventually.

After a while, minion-boy got to his feet and came to glare down at me with his hands on his hips. "You got food?" he asked.

I nodded and dug into my pockets. I handed over what I'd brought, half a stale loaf of bread, a rind of cheese, and a couple of raw potatoes I'd nicked off a cart in Sark Square. Minion-boy took it all and went back to his place by the stove. The other kids gathered around him as he shared out the food while the girl stuck the potatoes into the coals of the fire to cook them. After all the kids had taken their food, minion-boy came back and handed me a chunk of bread. I ate it slowly. Then he came back with a steaming potato. He squatted next to me and split it, handing me half.

I held the half potato cupped in my hands, warming my fingers. "Thanks," I said.

He nodded. "I'm Den." He pointed at the girl. "She's Jo. How come we never saw you before?"

"The old Underlord had a word out on me," I said.

"Crowe, you mean?" Den said.

I nodded, trying not to shiver at the sound of his name.

He took a bite of his potato. "Rough lot, Crowe. We didn't like him. But there's a new Underlord now, a better one. Embre-wing. He after you, too?"

He probably was. I shrugged.

"Looks like somebody beat the fluff out of you not too long ago," Den said. "You in trouble?"

I definitely was. I nodded.

The girl, Jo, came over and sat down beside big

Den. "Not very chatty, are you?"

"Not usually," I said. I took a bite of the potato. It wasn't all the way cooked in the middle and the skin was charred black. Still, it was better than Dawn Palace food.

"Well, we can't help you," Jo said, frowning. "Whatever trouble you're in."

I swallowed down the last of the potato. My stomach grumbled, wanting more. "I just need some information," I said.

"Yeah, I'll just bet you do," Den said, standing. He and Jo went back to their spot against the other wall. After a while, the other mudlark-kids quit picking through the trash, and rolled up together in their blankets, and Jo and Den wrapped up in their own ragged blankets, and the fire died down, leaving the small room dark with shadows.

I lay down on the dirt floor and went to sleep.

In the morning I woke up when somebody stepped over me and opened the door, spilling gray light into the room. Den. I got up and followed him outside.

The sky was covered with clouds that hung low and gray, but it wasn't raining. Den stood in the path with his hands on his hips. "What's your name?" he asked.

I rubbed the sleep out of my eyes. "Conn," I said.

"You a gutterboy?" Jo said from behind me.

I glanced over my shoulder. She stepped out of the shack's doorway and went to stand next to Den. They both looked me up and down.

"He's got a gutterboy name," Den said slowly. "And he looks like a gutterboy."

Jo shook her head. "But I don't think he is one."

"I *am* a—" I started.

And then I stopped. Because I wasn't anything like a gutterboy anymore. I'd run away to get some things done that I couldn't do if I was wearing fancy ducal magister clothes up in the Dawn Palace, and from the people who were trying to shut me into the ducal magister box.

But I missed those people, too, and I missed my

books and the warm sweater that Benet had knitted for me, and I missed Rowan, though I knew
she had to be furious with me, and I missed Nevery
even though he'd sent me away from Heartsease.

"I . . . used to be a gutterboy," I added slowly.
"But I'm something else now"—I didn't know what,
exactly—"and I need some information from you."

Den and Jo glanced at each other. Jo shrugged,
then Den nodded. "Right, Conn," Den said. "What
d'you want to know?"

I let out a breath. Good. "D'you know anything
about jewel thieves?" I asked.

CHAPTER 12

Den told me about a smokehole tavern on Strangle Street in the Twilight, a place where, he said, more than once he'd heard people whispering at a table in a corner about thievery and fancy jewels.

"But you don't want to get mixed up with that lot," Den told me.

I wasn't going to get mixed up with the locus stone thieves, I was just going to spy on them, and follow them to their headquarters, and see if I could figure out why they were stealing locus stones from the city's magisters. It was a strange thing for thieves to do, really, stealing locus stones. The thieves couldn't sell them, and if they weren't wizards they couldn't use them. It didn't make sense.

When it was late enough, I wound my way through the back alleys of the Twilight, followed by Pip-cat, to Strangle Street. There, I edged past a group of people gathered around a run-down shop with a broken front window, as if it'd had a brick thrown through it. Next to the shop was a burned-out husk of a house; the air smelled like smoke, as if the fire had happened recently. Trouble in the Twilight, but that was for Embre to deal with.

The smokehole was a tavern where people went to drink redstreak and black gin, and to make dark deals. I went down two steps and slunk inside the dim-dark room. Covering the floor was sawdust, scuffed up with damp patches. The walls were cracked plaster, and the ceiling was low. Along one wall was a counter, and behind that stood the tavern's keeper, a red-faced woman with burly arms. Around the room were rough wooden tables and benches, mostly empty.

I sat down at a table with my back against the wall and a clear path to the door. After a while the potboy, a kid wearing a stained apron and carrying a tray, came up to me.

"You got money to pay for that seat?" he asked, then wiped his nose with the back of his hand.

I nodded. I'd saved back a couple of coppers from selling my boots to the swagshop.

"A'right," the potboy said. "What d'you want?"

"Bread and cheese?" I asked.

"One copper lock," he said, and waited.

I gave him the coin; he went to fetch the food.

When he came back with a slice of bread and a piece of cheese, I nodded at the bench across from me. He glanced at the tavern keeper, then shrugged and sat down.

"Want some?" I asked, offering the plate.

He grabbed up the cheese and stuffed it into his mouth.

I took the plate back and ate a bite of the bread. "I'm looking for jewel thieves."

"Think you're going to find 'em here?" he asked, his mouth full.

I nodded.

The potboy glanced over his shoulder again. Then he swallowed down the cheese and leaned closer, whispering. "The chimney swifts. They drink at that table, late." He pointed at a table in the corner. "But you don't want to go in with them."

"Why not?" I asked.

He shrugged. "You just don't." He stood up. "And you can't hang about in here until they come in." He jerked his thumb toward the door. I left.

Chimney swifts! I should've thought of them before. They used their bristly brushes to sweep chimneys clean of soot, both in the Sunrise and the Twilight. *And* on the wizards' islands in the river. A chimney swift would make a very good thief. He or she could get into any house, even if the doors were locked, and steal something, then climb right back up the chimney again and be away clean.

But a chimney swift shouldn't be able to steal a wizard's locus magicalicus, because the stone would kill him if he touched it. That part about it was strange.

While I waited in an alley, I thought more about what I was. Not a gutterboy. Not the ducal magister. Something else. I was a wizard, and I was somebody all the other wizards in Wellmet except Nevery didn't like very much, and I knew the magics better than anyone. And I was Rowan's best friend and Embre's cousin, and they were the duchess and the Underlord, powerful people in Wellmet. What did all those things add up to, all together?

I thought about it, but I didn't come up with any answer.

So instead I thought about something more practical, how to spy on the chimney swifts. A long time ago, when Nevery had wanted to spy on the magisters, he'd done the embero spell on me and turned me into a cat because a cat makes a very good spy. I had a cat, Pip, but after the spying I couldn't turn Pip into a boy who could tell me what he'd seen and heard.

Hmmm. Maybe Pip *could* be my spy. Maybe I could do a spell so I could see through Pip's eyes and hear through its ears.

"Tallennar," I whispered. Pip-cat peered from around the side of the broken-down box it'd been hiding behind. After glaring at me for a moment, it padded over and crouched on the ground next to me.

"All right, Pip?" I said, and gave it a little scratch on the place between its ears. Its slowsilver fur wasn't soft; it felt prickly and made my fingers tingle.

Pip-cat rubbed its face against my hand—friends again—then climbed up my front and onto my shoulder. Its cat tail prickled where it rested against the back of my neck.

After thinking about it for a while, remembering

words in the spell language, I reached up and rested my hand on Pip's back.

"Magics," I said in the magical-spell dragon language. "Please make this work without . . . without . . ."

As I spoke, the magics shifted, and I felt it the moment they turned their attention onto tiny me—like looking into the night sky and having the stars look back. Immense, powerful, a little frightening. The air around me stilled and my ears popped. "Magics," I went on, my voice sounding thin in the echoing silence. "Please make this spell work without hurting Pip." I took a breath. "Or me," I added quickly, and then I launched into my made-up eyes-and-ears spell.

The spell tingled in the air, hanging like a sparkling cloud in front of me, then the magics shifted and I heard a roaring thunder inside my head as the spell focused itself into a glowing blue spark bright enough to burn. The spark exploded in front of Pip's eyes and then in front of mine, and crashed into Pip's ears and then into mine, clattering around inside my skull as if it was scouring out my brain.

Catching my breath, I blinked the brights out of my eyes and shook my head. Everything looked ordinary—gray sky, muddy ground, brick alley wall at my back, Pip-cat crouched on my shoulder. Then, to finish, I added Pip's true name to the spell, "*Tallennar.*"

The world spun and flashed and I closed my eyes quick—and everything changed. With my newly sensitive Pip-ears I heard the *rush-rush-rush* of the river, and the rustle of a pigeon's wings on the roof far overhead, and the wind blowing across the top of a chimney, and a man talking to himself two streets over. Carefully I cracked open my eyes, squinting against the brightness. Pip looked down and through its keen eyes I saw the dirty cobblestones, every bump and crack outlined in glowing sparks. Pip turned its head and looked at me, and I saw myself, a gutterboy-wizard with a dirt-smudged face and wide blue eyes, and a cloud of crackling fire around him. So that's what I looked like to a dragon.

"*Connwaer*," I whispered. I watched the gutter-boy's lips move. A flash in front of my eyes and a roaring in my ears, and I saw and heard as my ordinary self again, the ordinary Pip sitting next to me.

I peered around. Nobody had noticed; I was still alone in the dim-dark alley.

Well. The spell had effected with more power than I'd ever felt before. It wouldn't be temporary, either; I'd have the use of Pip's eyes and ears anytime I needed them, just by saying Pip's true name. It was a good spell. A very, very good spell.

I slept for a while in the alley, curled up behind a pile of trash. After midnight, I woke up and went back to the smokehole tavern. Seeing me come in, the potboy nodded, then pointed with his chin toward a dark corner. At a table sat three men and a woman, all wearing black clothes, all smudged with soot. From the doorway I looked them over carefully. None of them were the men who'd beaten the fluff out of me but they were chimney swifts, sure as sure. My plan was to sit at a table near them and use Pip to listen to their conversation, and then to follow them to wherever they lived.

One of the swifts was thin and small enough that he looked like he might squeeze himself into a narrow chimney and then get stuck, but the other two men and the woman were bigger and burlier, more like minions. None of them did go up chimneys themselves, I realized. Whenever you saw a swift in the streets, walking to a job, he always had a soot-smudged kid following him, a boy or girl dressed in black, carrying one of the bristly brushes or a bag. *They* were the ones who went up the chimneys. The kids were the ones doing the stealing, then, working on the swifts' orders.

I could go up a chimney, couldn't I? And I was a very good thief.

I knew what Nevery would say. *Don't be stupid, boy.* He'd want me to be *safe* and *careful*. But careful wouldn't get done what I needed to do. Sure as sure, this was a better way than sneaking and spying to find out what I needed from the chimney swifts.

Pip slunk under a nearby bench and I walked up to the swifts' table. The four of them sat with their heads down, leaning forward, talking in low whispers. Seeing me, they broke off.

"What d'you want?" asked a long-faced man with red-rimmed eyes. He took a drink of ale and wiped the back of his hand across his mouth, leaving a clean patch in his sooty face.

"Never mind what he wants," said the woman, who wore a black woolen dress with a black shawl over her broad shoulders. "Take yerself off, boy." She pointed at the smokehole door.

The four turned back to their conversation, but I stood there waiting.

They gave me narrow-eyed, sidelong glances, then the woman whispered something to the burly man across from her. He nodded, put his hands on the table, and pushed himself to his feet, then climbed over his bench and reached for me. Before he could grab me and throw me out the door, I ducked under his reaching hands and said, in a loud whisper, *"Locus stones."*

The four of them stared at me, looking around to see if anybody else in the tavern had heard.

The burly man held me by the scruff of my neck, standing behind me like a wall. The woman grabbed me by the front of my ragged vest and jerked me closer to the table. "What d'you know about locus stones, gutterboy?" she hissed.

I couldn't shrug because burly-man had a tight grip on me from behind. "I know you steal 'em," I whispered. "And I could steal 'em, too."

The woman's eyes narrowed. "How'd you manage that?" she asked.

"I have quick hands," I said.

The fourth man at the table, the skinniest one, leaned forward. "What d'you want, gutterboy?"

"What d'you think?" I asked.

From behind, burly-man gave me a rough shake. "Answer," he growled.

Right. "I'm a thief," I said. "I want to be a chimney swift."

"Huh," the woman said, and let me go. Burly-man kept his grip on my scruff. "You want to work for us, you mean?"

I nodded.

She looked past me at burly-man. "What d'you think, Drury?" she asked.

He let go of my scruff and grabbed my arm. "We take him to Sootle, is what."

The others got up from the table and, dragging me with them, went out the door of the smokehole tavern and into the dark streets of the Twilight.

On the way out, I saw the potboy staring, and then shaking his head.

But I wasn't worried. This was a very good plan.

CHAPTER 13

I figured Sootle, the chimney swifts' leader, would be hiding out in the Twilight somewhere, but the four swifts hustled me through the dark and deserted streets and down to the bank of the river, where they shoved me into a rowboat. Two of them, the woman and the burly man, Drury, got in; the other two stayed behind on the shore.

So did Pip. The cat-dragon would find me on the other side of the river. Hopefully Pip would come soon, just in case I needed to do the dazzler spell or the needle-prickler to get away from the swifts.

Drury rowed the boat across the river, past the dark and sleeping magisters' islands. Heartsease was dark, too, except for one light shining from a window on the second floor. *Hello, Nevery*, I thought as the boat slipped silently past the island. He was up late, working in the study, reading a book or writing in his grimoire. If he could see me now he'd be furious, most likely, and so would Benet. So would Embre and Rowan and Kerrn, for that matter. They didn't need to worry. Sure as sure I could look after myself.

On the other side of the river, Drury and the woman, whose name was Floss, led me down the Sunrise streets and 'round the back of a plain-fronted house and took me inside. They put me in a room and told me to wait, which I did for a long time. I listened to the tromping sound of feet in a room upstairs, and then I lay on the hard floor and fell asleep. Finally they came back and brought me down a long hallway and up some stairs and into a dim-dark room.

Three chimney swifts were sitting around a plain table with a lit candle on it. I looked carefully at them, just in case any of them were the men who'd tried to kidnap me from the Heartsease courtyard, but I'd never seen any of them before.

In the room, heavy curtains hung over the windows, and the rest of the room was empty, not even any pictures on the walls or carpets on the floor. A fireplace gaped like an empty mouth, no fire burning there. The swifts ignored us as we came in.

One of them pointed up at the ceiling. "He coming down again, Sootle?" he asked the man sitting at the end of the table.

Sootle was tall and very thin and he had a pointy nose and long, black, stringy hair with a bald patch on the top of his head; and, like the others, he was smudged with soot. "No, we're done. The men he brought in will take care of the rest of it," he said.

"Take yourselves off. Looks like I've got some other business here."

The other chimney swifts went out of the room, leaving me facing Sootle, with Drury and Floss standing behind me, blocking the door.

"Well?" Sootle asked. He looked me up and down with sharp, black eyes. "You've brought me a gutterboy, have you?"

"Says he knows about stolen wizard stones," Floss said.

Sootle's sharp eyes narrowed. "What d'you know exactly, gutterboy?"

I shrugged.

The sooty hand flashed out and he cuffed me across the face. "I asked you a question, gutterboy. Answer it."

Shaking off the blow, I nodded. "I figured out about the stones. And I want to come work for you."

"Do you, now? We'll see about that. What's your name?" Sootle asked.

"Pip," I said. It was the first name I could think

of that wasn't my own.

"You afraid to go up a chimney, Pip?" asked Sootle.

"No," I said. I didn't think I was. "I'm a lock-pick, too," I added quickly.

"Are you, then?" Sootle drummed his long fingers on the tabletop. "What d'you think, Floss? Drury?"

Floss stepped back to look me over. "He's too tall," she said.

Sootle nodded. "He's skinny, though. He might do. I might take him on myself. I could use an intrepid lockpicker charboy like this, especially after last night." He got to his feet, then went to the hearth, where he squatted down, leaned into the fireplace, and looked up. "Flue's open." He stood. "Up you go, young Pip. Tell us about the view from the top."

Up the chimney, he meant. All right. I went over to the fireplace and ducked inside. The brick walls of the chimney closed around me, burned black and a little wider than my shoulders. I looked up. Spiderwebs and darkness, and at the very top— way, way above—a square of dark gray, the night sky with morning coming soon.

How was I supposed to climb all the way up there?

"Get on with it, Pip," came Sootle's hollow voice from outside. "Or I'll light a fire under you."

I slid my hands along the walls. Flat bricks, gritty with soot, and then, just over my head, a brick sticking out a little farther than the others. A ledge. For climbing up! I looked and found some other ledges lower down. Kicking off my shoes and my one sock and leaving them at the bottom, I started climbing. My toes clung to the sticking-out bricks and my fingers gripped hard, pulling me up. The chimney closed in around me like a dark square tunnel, growing narrower as I went higher. Soot crumbled from the bricks and sifted down, and rubbed off as my shoulders and knees brushed the walls. I heard a *rush-rush-rush* of wind blowing over the top of the chimney and felt the air pull at me, just as it pulled the smoke up from the hearth.

I kept climbing, blinking to keep the soot out of my eyes, coughing when I breathed it in. At last, panting with the effort, I got to the top, where I pulled myself up, hooked my arms over the edge of the chimney, and looked around, catching my breath. Off to the east the sky was just turning the pink and gray of morning. The dark slate rooftops of the Sunrise lay all around me, chimneys sticking out of them like snaggled teeth, most of them leaking smudges of smoke. Some of them had birds' nests built on them.

Wind whistled over the rooftops, ruffling my hair. I could see so far! The Dawn Palace loomed over the Sunrise from its hilltop, glimmering pink in the morning light.

I waved at the palace, at the ducal magister's stuffy rooms and his closet full of fancy clothes and his cold cabbage soup, and his bag full of money. "Hello, Ro!" I shouted. With Rowan so busy, she was probably already hunched over her desk with Miss Dimity hovering over her like a vulture. I knew Rowan—she'd rather be taking a sword-fighting lesson than getting ready to go to another boring meeting. For a moment I felt sorry for her, stuck in her duchess box.

Below the palace, the city was starting to stir. I turned and looked in the other direction, toward the shadowy dark of the Twilight. In the dusty-dim light the river gleamed like slowsilver, flowing around the wizards' islands, under the Night Bridge, and away. I took a deep breath and let it out. I felt like I could leap from the chimney and fly over the city like a black bird, free and light.

From the corner of my eye I caught a glimpse of something moving, and jerked my head around to look. A cat, lurking.

"Hello, Pip," I said, grinning. Pip bounded across the rooftiles, crawled up the outside of the chimney, and crouched next to me.

From below I heard a hollow shout. Oh, right.

The swifts were down there waiting for me, and Sootle, who thought I might be frightened of climbing up a chimney.

Still grinning, I started down, skiffing from one brick-edge to the next, to the bottom, where I landed in a cloud of soot. I ducked out of the fireplace and stood.

"Well?" Sootle asked. He and Floss and Drury had been waiting, and not very patiently, by the looks of it.

I swiped at the soot on my face. "The sun's rising," I said. "And I could see all the way to the Twilight from up there."

From the chimney came a scrabbling noise, and more soot sifted down. The swifts stared as Pip, covered with soot so it was completely black, dropped down into the fireplace and crawled out into the room. Its eyes gleamed red and it glared around, its tail twitching. Seeing me, it padded over, then climbed up to my shoulder.

"What is *that*?" Sootle asked, backing away a

step when Pip turned its head to look at him.

"It's a cat," I said.

They stared.

Krrrr, Pip said.

"It's purring, see?" I said. Pip opened its mouth in a yawn, showing a row of needle-sharp teeth. "It likes chimneys," I said. And so did I.

Floss glanced at Sootle. "He'll do, then?" she asked.

"He'll do," Sootle said. He looked me over again with his sharp black eyes. "And I've got just the job for him."

CHAPTER 14

Before Sootle told me what just-the-job he had for me, he took me down to the house's cellar to meet the other chimney swift kids, seven of them, one for each swift. They were called charboys and chargirls, and they looked like they'd been charred; they were dressed in black and covered with soot from their hair to their bare feet. They were just waking up, blinking in the light of the lantern that Sootle carried down the cellar steps. The cellar didn't look too bad. It was damp, but every kid had a woolen blanket.

"You'll sleep here, Pip," Sootle said to me. Then we headed back up the stairs, the charkids following, to the kitchen at the back of the house, where he left me. Another chimney swift was stirring a pot of porridge. Eggs were frying in a pan on the stove. As the kids came in, the swift gave each one a bowl of porridge with an egg on top. He gave one to me, too. We sat down on the floor and ate it with our fingers and wiped our faces on our sleeves. Pip came and sat next to me and I gave it some of my egg to eat.

The charboys and girls didn't say anything, they just watched me and Pip with their pale eyes in their sooty faces, slurping up their egg-and-porridge. They were like the gutterkids and mudlarks. All they thought about was chimneys and what they were going to have for dinner. They didn't have anybody to look after them, I realized. Not like I did. These kids were so busy looking after themselves that they didn't have time for anything else.

I'd been just like that before I'd picked Nevery's pocket and become a wizard.

"D'you know how to read, any of you?" I asked.

One of them shook her head, the others just stared.

When we were finished, Sootle came back and brought me to the door. Taking out a purse string, he pulled off a couple of copper lock coins, which he handed to me. "Go to a swagshop, Pip, and get yourself some proper charboy clothes. Black." He narrowed his dark eyes. Was he smiling? "So the soot won't show." He shoved me out the door. "Be back by midday."

Right. I skiffed off. I'd get the charboy clothes, but I had some other things to do first.

Nevery was *not* happy to see me. It was still early morning when I snuck into Heartsease, and he hadn't had his tea yet.

Leaving Pip-cat outside to hunt pigeons, I went into the study. From his chair, Nevery glared at me. "When was the last time you had a wash?"

I was filthy, true. I was very glad to see him, too. "I went up a chimney, Nevery."

"Hmph," he said. "I suppose you enjoyed that, my lad."

I grinned at him. Sure as sure, it'd been better than any Dawn Palace meeting.

Nevery opened his mouth to scold me some more when Benet came in, carrying a tray with tea things on it. Seeing me, he stopped and set the tray down on the table with a thump. "You'll need another cup," he growled.

I remembered the errand Sootle had sent me on. "Benet, can I have my black sweater back?"

Benet grunted and went out.

Nevery poured me a cup of tea and I fetched it and went to sit on the hearth. Benet brought another teacup and saucer and my black sweater, then went out, making sure I got more glare before he left.

I took off the tattered vest and pulled the sweater on over my head. There, now I felt more like myself.

The tea was good and hot. I blew on it to cool it and took a sip. Lady-the-cat came in and, purring, climbed onto my lap. I sighed, happy to be home.

I knew, though, that this wouldn't actually *be* my home again until I figured out what I was, me the gutterboy-wizard-apprentice-ducal-magister-magical-thief.

"Well?" Nevery asked impatiently, pouring out his own tea and adding honey. "What have you been up to, Connwaer?"

Right. "I found out who's been stealing the locus stones." While petting Lady, I told him about the chimney swifts and how they could go down a chimney, steal a stone, and climb back out again, easy.

"Chimney *swifts?*" Nevery asked, when I finished.

I nodded.

"Swifts," he muttered. He got to his feet and went to the bookshelf, then pulled out a book and glanced through the pages. "Ah." He set the book on the table. "Come here and look at this."

I set Lady aside and went to the table. It was a book about birds. Nevery's finger tapped the page, showing me where to look. The page said, *Chimney Swift, known to nest in chimneys and on rooftops.*

Then a picture of a black bird with sleek wings and a forked tail. I stared at it and my stomach turned cold. "A swift is a kind of black bird?"

Nevery sat in his chair again. "You didn't know?"

No, I didn't.

"Black birds, Conn," he said. "The chimney swifts could have something to do with Crowe."

Could they? My name, Connwaer, meant a kind of black bird, and so did Embre's—he was really Embre-wing, a black bird with a bright orange spot on its wings. My mother's name had been Black Maggie, or Magpie. We had those names because we were part of the same family. So was Crowe.

"Boy, I've had this feeling"—Nevery shook his head—"a feeling that some kind of plot is taking shape around us. I think it's possible that Crowe has returned out of exile."

Just the thought of that made fright shiver through me. Then I considered it. "No, Nevery," I said. "It's not him. Embre and I thought maybe Crowe sent those men who beat the fluff out of me, so I did the anstriker spell to look for him. Crowe's not in Wellmet."

"The anstriker spell, hmm? You're sure? The spell worked, even with the magics in such disorder?"

I nodded. "Those two fluff-beaters who came after me weren't swifts, either. It's all right, Nevery."

"It is not *all right*, boy." Nevery frowned at me. "I don't like this sneaking around."

Oh, he was going to like this even less. "That's not exactly what I'm doing," I admitted. "I've joined the chimney swifts. Their leader has taken me on as his charboy."

"Curse it!" Nevery slammed his fist on the table. His teacup jumped in its saucer and then tipped over, spilling tea across the tabletop. "Curse it," he muttered again, and blotted up spilled tea with his sleeve. "This is too dangerous. You've identified the thieves; now it's time to send in the palace guard to deal with them."

That was a terrible idea. "But Nevery, I haven't found out anything yet. I don't know how they're stealing locus stones without the stones killing them, and I don't know why they're stealing the stones in the first place." Captain Kerrn's guards wouldn't find that out, either. They'd just go stomping around in their boots making a lot of noise, and most likely the swifts would get away and the stolen locus stones would be lost. "I need to be a charboy for a little longer, just until I find out what the swifts are up to."

Nevery frowned at me from under his bushy eyebrows. After a long moment he righted his cup, poured himself more tea, and stirred in some honey. *Tink-tink-tink* went the spoon on the side of the cup.

"Another locus stone went missing last night, boy," he said. "Sandera's—again. The thefts are a serious problem, some sort of attack on the magisters of the city." He set down the spoon. "Conn, I do see the necessity in pursuing this. But you must be more careful."

"Nevery, I am—"

"No." Nevery pointed at me. "You're not." He sighed and rubbed his hand across his face. All of a sudden he looked weary and gray. What was making him look so old? "And the two-magic problem is getting worse," he added.

I nodded. "You can feel it, too?"

He snorted. "Every wizard in the city can feel it, Connwaer. The thieves have stolen these locus stones at the time when the city most needs its wizards. The magisters have prohibited the use of magic by all the wizards in the city—with the magics this unsettled, spells may effect in more and more dangerous ways." He lowered his eyebrows. "You know how bad things could get, my lad."

I did. If the magics stayed like this for much longer, it'd mean worse than just a few spells gone wrong.

"The magisters blame you for all of this, of course," Nevery said.

I knew that. "Don't worry, Nevery," I said, getting to my feet. "I'll go out now and talk to the magics and see if I can help them." It's what I'd been meaning to do, until the chimney swifts had distracted me. It had to be me because none of the other wizards—except Nevery—truly understood that the magics were actual beings, not just power that was there to be used, and none of them had quite realized that their magical spells were actually the magics' language—that by saying a spell we were talking to the magics.

"Will you, indeed?" he asked, leaning back in his chair. "Then I will go with you."

I knew better than to argue. Once Nevery made up his mind to do something, he'd do it.

We could do it right here, at Heartsease island.

Now that I thought about it, Heartsease was in between the Sunrise and the Twilight—the best place for dealing with the magics, really.

Outside, the cobbled courtyard was clotted with white, smoky fog mixed with the yellowish mist that crept up from the river and hung low to the ground. Nevery swept-stepped across the courtyard, and the fog swirled out of his way and closed in again behind us.

I reached out and tugged on Nevery's sleeve. "Over here," I said, and pointed past the tall, bare-branched tree. We came to the edge of the courtyard, climbed over a low tumble of rocks, and stood on the muddy bank of the river. The water was smooth under the fog, and lapping quietly against the shore; farther out it flowed swiftly and silently past. In the dim light I caught glimpses of the Twilight shore; I could see cranes poking out above the fog and the dark hulls of a couple of ships at anchor.

Nevery stepped up beside me, looking out at the foggy river. "Explain how we're going to do this *talking* to the magics, boy," he said, "and tell me, too, what you're planning to talk to them about."

I hadn't had time to think it through. "Well, Nevery," I said slowly, figuring it out as I talked. "When Arhionvar came here to Wellmet, we could have banished it, but instead we let it stay."

"*We*, is it?" Nevery said, but he was pulling at the end of his beard, so I knew he wasn't really angry.

"Well, I did," I admitted. "What I did was, I used slowsilver to tie both magics to the city. The problem is that the Arhionvar magic is sort of young and strong and way more powerful than our old, tired Wellmet magic."

He nodded; he knew that as well as I did.

"I think the magical beings are bound together by the magic that I did, and they're fighting each other at the same time to be the magic of the city. So when a wizard here does a spell, they both try to effect it, and the spell turns out all wrong, or it turns out twice as strong as the wizard expected it to be."

"Hmm. So how do you plan to fix that problem?"

I nodded. "I wonder if they'd both be happier"—
I stopped because I wasn't sure the magics even *felt*
happiness the way we did—"if they'd feel more
settled, I mean, if they each took a different part
of the city for themselves. Arhionvar could have the
Sunrise and the old Wellmet magic could have the
Twilight."

Nevery glanced sideways at me and pulled his
locus magicalicus out of his cloak pocket. "Interesting,
and it may work. Show me what to do."

Nevery didn't know the spellwords to do this.
But his locus magicalicus, joined with mine, would
make my voice clearer to the magic. "Pip," I called.

Pip-cat bounded over from where it'd been poking its whiskers into a pile of riverweed and trash
and climbed up to perch on my shoulder. I rested
my hand on its paw.

Speaking slowly, I started the spell, saying hello to
the magics and reminding them who I was and telling them that Nevery was here with me. In response,
the magics gathered around us, making everything

turn white-bright with flames and sparks. I smelled the dry, smoky smell of pyrotechnics, and my skin prickled all over. Nevery's locus magicalicus gave a sudden bright flash.

"The magics know you," I gasped.

Nevery gave a brisk nod and kept a tight grip on his locus stone.

I spoke a few more spellwords and the magics grew brighter, crackling through my bones and sparking off my skin. Then my ears popped and everything went silent, as if we were floating in a bubble. I blinked. We were still standing near the river, tall, gray-robed Nevery and small, ragged Connwaer with a bright spark of a cat-dragon on his shoulder, but overlaying my vision was the magics' view. Everything looked tiny, far away, the city a dark, flowing plain, Nevery, Pip, and me blazing like bright stars at the edge of Heartsease island, the other wizards of the city duller sparks. The slow-silver that flowed beneath the river kept the magics attached to this place with a bone-deep pull.

The first time I'd talked to the magics like this, when I'd settled Arhionvar in the city, they didn't want to let me go, and I hadn't found myself again for a long time. This time, especially with Nevery with me, I had to be extra careful.

Keeping my hand on Pip's paw, speaking slowly in the dragon language, I asked the Arhionvar magic if it would be the great wall and power of the Sunrise, and I showed it the river, a barrier that it could not cross. Then I told the Wellmet magic that it could care for the Twilight.

The magics talked back. We couldn't hear them with our ears; their voices rumbled in our bones, surrounding us with light and sound. They were like the huge shadows of dragons, if shadows were made of pure lightning and thunder. Slowly, with the feeling of enormous stones shifting, Arhionvar gathered itself and settled like a blanket of brilliant stars over the Sunrise. Glowing softly, the Wellmet magic eased gently into its own place over the Twilight.

There. Done. Settled.

I spoke the last words of the spell.

The magics were supposed to let me go, then—that's what the spell had asked them to do—but they kept their grip on me, swirling around me and pulling me away. They wanted me to be with them. At first, when I was a gutterboy thief, they had wanted me because I'd been alone, like them, and now, I guessed, they noticed me most because I had a dragon locus stone. They wanted me to become part of them, too huge and dragonish and too full of light to see or remember tiny Nevery or Benet or Rowan, or anyone in Wellmet. I gasped for breath against the pressure; my feet lifted off the ground.

Nevery's hand came down solid on my shoulder, steadying me, and maybe himself, too. His deep voice rang out, speaking sharp, spell-ending words.

The magics clung to me for a breath, then another, then *snap*—they let me go. The heavy, pressing weight of Arhionvar lifted, and the warmth of the old Wellmet magic seeped away.

The bubble of silence around us popped, and we were left standing on the muddy riverbank, cold mist swirling around our ankles.

I lifted my heavy hand off of Pip's paw, blinked, and found Nevery holding tightly to my shoulder. Pip dropped off my other shoulder and landed splat on the ground. I staggered a bit and Nevery let me go, and I sat down. He leaned heavily on his cane. With a shaking hand, he put his locus magicalicus back into his cloak pocket.

I rubbed my hand across my eyes. That'd been close. Too close.

Nevery cleared his throat. When he spoke, his voice sounded rusty. "So that's what happened when we lost you before."

I nodded. When I'd brought Arhionvar into the city, the magics had taken me and hadn't given me back for a long time. I shivered, remembering it.

Tendrils of cold crept in with the fog. I picked up Pip, who was shivering, too, and climbed to my feet; then I snuggled Pip up against my woolly black sweater. Might as well test to see that it had worked. "*Minnervas,*" I whispered, and the spell effected exactly as it was supposed to. The little cat-Pip started to glow with warmth, clinging to the front of my sweater with its claws. I breathed out a sigh of relief.

"Hmph." Nevery turned and led the way back onto the courtyard. "Well done, my lad," he said.

I glowed a little from his words, too. "Thanks, Nevery."

"But you know, Connwaer," he added over his shoulder. "It is not a bad thing to ask for help now and then."

He paused and I caught up to him. "What d'you mean?" I asked.

"You don't have to do everything yourself," Nevery said. "Ask for help and perhaps you won't get yourself into so much trouble."

Duchess Rowan—

It is as we suspected. Conn has disguised himself as a gutterboy and has discovered who has been stealing the locus stones. He has joined the thieves in order to learn why, exactly, they are taking locus magicalicus stones. I fear Conn is putting himself into further danger, but short of having Captain Kerrn lock him up in one of the Dawn Palace cells, there is nothing we can do about it.

Now that Brumbee, Trammel, Nimble, and Sandera's stones have been stolen, it has become clear that this is a targeted attack against the magisters. The apprentice Keeston's stone must have been stolen as a trial run by the thieves. Though I am worried for Conn's safety, he does have a point that, as both a wizard and a former thief, he is the best person to discover what is really going on. I recommend that we do as Underlord Embre suggested, and let Conn get on with it.

Nevery Flinglas
Magister, Heartsease, etc.

CHAPTER 15

That afternoon, Sootle put two bulgy burlap bags into a boat and rowed us over to one of the magisters' islands. I carried one of the bags and he carried the other, and, followed by Pip, we went 'round the back of the house to the servants' door, where the housekeeper let us in.

"Right this way," she said, leading

us down a long corridor. "The fires is all out, on account of you swifts coming today. The one in here's been smoking something terrible." She led us to a fancy bedroom, and I realized whose house it was. The carpet on the floor was spangled with little blue flowers, and a painting of a family crest—more blue flowers—hung over the fireplace. Periwinkle, one of the magisters, lived here.

Outside, Sootle had told me about the job. "We go in, we sweep the chimneys, we get paid, we leave. When you go up top, check the layout, be sure you can get in the chimney from outside."

Then he'd handed me a piece of chalk and told me what to do with it.

In Periwinkle's bedroom, Sootle pulled a wire-bristle brush from one of the bags and handed it to me, checked to see the flue was open, and sent me up the chimney. I was to go up top first, then sweep out the soot on the way down. The soot would fall into the hearth and Sootle would catch it in a canvas cloth he'd spread there.

Up I went. Pip came, too, crawling up the bricks ahead of me, sending ticks of soot down into my face. The chimney grew narrower as I went up, squeezing my shoulders. My knees got sore from pressing against the bricks as I climbed. At last, coughing soot out of my lungs, I reached the top. Something was blocking the way. I reached up and felt twigs and straw—a nest. No wonder the chimney smoked. I pushed it aside and poked my head out. The nest—a swift nest, it must be—was empty, so I let it fall onto the rooftiles. Pip perched next to me on the edge of the chimney. I looked out and saw another seven chimneys poking up from the sloped rooftop. Would I have to sweep them all?

Holding the brush with one hand, I groped in my pocket for the chalk, pulled it out, and reached over the side of the chimney and marked the bricks with an X.

On the way down, I brushed choking clouds of soot off the walls.

"Do it again," Sootle said, when I reached the

bottom and climbed out. "Not enough soot. You haven't scrubbed it well enough."

Back up I went, all the way to the top, and on the way down scraped even more soot off the chimney bricks. Then I did another chimney, and another one. Coughing up black soot, I reached the bottom of the fourth chimney, this one in a dining room, and Sootle was sitting in a chair unwrapping bacon and cheese in two slices of bread.

Oh, good. Time to eat. My stomach growled.

"None for you, Pip," Sootle said. "You had a good breakfast, and we don't want our charboys getting fat. You'd get stuck up there, wouldn't you?"

I didn't think I would.

Sootle took a bite of his cheese-and-bacon. "Back up with you," he said, his mouth full. "And do it proper-like this time."

I took a deep breath and headed back up the chimney.

By the time we got to the last chimney, the eighth one, my arms and legs were quivering with tiredness and my fingers and toes were rubbed raw from clinging to the bricks. My eyes burned and every breath felt clogged with soot. I sat on the doorstep and coughed while the housekeeper paid Sootle. He threaded the coins onto a purse string and handed me a bag to carry.

That job was done, but the just-the-job was still waiting to be done. In the dead of night I was asleep in the charkids' cellar, Pip-cat curled next to me, when a bony hand shook me awake. "Up with you, Pip," Sootle's voice said. He held a lantern turned low. Blinking, I followed him up the stairs into the dark, empty kitchen. "We've got a chimney to sweep," he whispered.

A chimney to sweep in the middle of the night?

Without speaking, we left the house, winding our way through the quiet, dark streets of the Sunrise to the river. Sootle rowed us out to the magisters' island, to Periwinkle's house. There he tied the boat, then led me 'round the side of the house, which was a dark shadow against the darker night, no lights showing. Nobody awake inside, then.

Two other chimney swifts, Drury and the skinny one from the smokehole tavern, were waiting there. Sootle whispered with them while I yawned and rubbed sleep out of my eyes. The river flowed past with a quiet *rush-rush*, and the stars shone down. Over the island I felt the magics of the city, the stone strength of Arhionvar pushing up against the warmth of the old Wellmet magic. Still settled. Pip-cat climbed up to my shoulder and crouched there, its prickle-fluff tail curled around my neck like a scarf.

Sootle pulled me by the sleeve and I followed him to the side of the house. A rope ladder hung there. "Up," Sootle breathed into my ear. "And quiet as you go."

I started up, Pip climbing the stone wall beside me. I felt the ladder jerk, and then Sootle started up, too. I glanced over my shoulder and saw him below me, a dark lump against the side of the house.

At the top, Pip and I crouched at the edge of the roof until Sootle joined us. He had a knapsack on his back. "Which chimney?" he whispered.

Which one had I marked with the chalk that day, he meant.

The eight chimneys stuck up from the roof like dead tree trunks, all of them the same. "I think it's that one," I whispered, pointing.

We climbed the sloping roof, the overlapping slate tiles cool and rough under my bare feet, to the chimney. Drats. No chalk-marked X on the bricks.

We checked another chimney, and then another, and found the mark, pale white in the starlight. My feet crunched on sticks, the remains of the swift's nest I'd pushed off the chimney that morning.

"Shh," Sootle breathed. He pulled me down to crouch next to him, right beside the chimney.

Right. Now what?

Sootle took off his knapsack and set it on the roof. "Here's what you're going to do, Pip," he whispered. He pulled a long, rag-wrapped package out

of the knapsack. "Torryfine tongs," he whispered.
"Use them to pick up the lady wizard's locus stone.
It'll be next to her bed, or somewhere nearby. It looks
like an ordinary river stone." He gripped me by the
front of my black sweater and pulled me closer, his
voice hissing into my ear. "Whatever happens, *don't
touch the stone*. It'll kill you dead if you do, and that
wouldn't do us much good, would it?"

I shook my head.

He let me go and pulled another package out of
the knapsack and unwrapped it. A cage made out of
wire mesh, about the size of my hand. In the starlight, the cage wires glimmered pearly green.

"It's made of torryfine metal," Sootle whispered.
"Use the tongs to put the wizard stone in here, and
it won't hurt you. Then come back up."

Torryfine? *Tourmalifine*, he meant. The little
cage and the tongs were made out of tourmalifine.

That meant . . .

Oh, it was clever! Tourmalifine repelled magic;
I'd read all about that. This was how the chimney
swifts were stealing and hiding the locus stones

without getting killed by them. Because tourmali-fine repelled magic, the tongs and the cage protected the thief from the effects of touching a locus magicalicus. Had Sootle thought that up himself?

He put the rag-wrapped tongs and cage into the knapsack and handed it to me. "My other charboy lost his nerve," Sootle said. "Nearly bunged things up last night thieving another lady wizard's stone. He's no use to me anymore. You going to be useful, my intrepid young Pip?"

I nodded.

"Right, then," he whispered. "Off you go."

Right. I slung the knapsack on my back and climbed into the chimney.

Down I went, my arms and legs aching from all the sweeping I'd done earlier in the day. As I went lower, the bricks grew warmer and the air grew thick with smoke. Looking down the shaft of the chimney, I saw below me the red glow of a dying fire in the hearth. A cough tickled in my throat, and I covered my face with my sweater-sleeve and choked it back down again. Pip climbed past me, flicking me in the face with its tail. I blinked the smoke out of my eyes and watched as Pip-cat climbed down to the hearth and then snapped up the dying embers, swallowing them until only ash was left and the smoke cleared.

Well done, Pip. I climbed the rest of the way down. At the bottom, I lowered myself quietly into the ashy hearth. I crouched there, surveying the room. Pip crouched next to me, its red eyes glowing.

The room was completely dark. The wide, canopied bed was against one wall, I knew, and there was a wardrobe and another chair somewhere around, and a small table that I didn't want to bump into. I didn't dare use the lothfalas spell to kindle a light.

Oh, but I did have a way to see better.

I rested my hand on Pip's back and, my voice the barest breath of a whisper, said *"Tallennar,"* and blinked, and through Pip's eyes the room was shining with light, everything in it edged with ember-bright flame. I heard with Pip's ears, too, the wind *rush-shush*ing over the top of the chimney, way overhead, and the soft huffs of the sleeper in the bed, breathing.

As I lifted Pip onto my shoulder, the room shifted and I saw the room from my level. There, the table beside the bed. Sure as sure, the locus stone was there. My feet feather quiet, I crept out of the hearth and across the room. On the table, a stack of books, a dark werelight lantern, and no locus stone. It was more a cabinet than a table, I realized. I crouched down. There, a door. In Pip's fire-vision its keyhole sparkled.

I had just the thing for it. I fished my lockpick wires out of my pocket and—*quick hands*—picked the sparking lock. The door swung open, silent. Inside, on a little velvet pillow, was a locus magicalicus stone. It was a plain, rounded, gray river stone, but to Pip's eyes it burned brighter than a star, a blaze of dazzling light in the dark cave of the cabinet.

I didn't bother with the tourmalifine tongs. I already knew I could touch the locus stone without being hurt by it. I reached in to pick it up. Then I froze, my fingers not quite touching the stone, the light from it so bright I could see the dark shadows of my bones inside the glowing skin of my hand.

Should I do this? Steal a locus stone from a wizard? I'd done it once before, when I'd been a gutterboy and had picked Nevery's pocket. Then, I hadn't known what I was doing. Now I did. I knew what it was like for a wizard to lose a locus magicalicus.

It was awful. When I'd lost my first locus magicalicus, it'd been like being desperately hungry and never finding a bite of something to eat. A horrible, empty, aching feeling.

But I had to do this. My hand shook a little as I lowered it and picked up the stone. My fingers tingled, and the stone flashed, filling the room with sudden light. It was light that only Pip could see, and me, seeing through Pip's eyes.

Blinking the brights out of my eyes, I paused, listening. The sleeper in the bed didn't stir.

I pulled the tourmalifine cage out of the knapsack and unwrapped it. The wires felt cold. I put the locus stone inside the cage. As it touched the wires, the stone snapped and flared, giving off sparks and sizzles of magic. It didn't like being in there. Quickly I wrapped it back up again. Then I crept back across the room to the chimney. After whispering the spell to get my own vision and hearing back, I climbed up, the knapsack scraping against the brick walls. At the top I climbed out.

Sootle was waiting. "You've got it?" he whispered.

I crouched next to him beside the chimney, and nodded. Yes, I had it. Periwinkle's locus magicalicus. "What're you going to do with it?" I asked.

Sootle gave me a keen look. "None of your business, is it?"

True, it wasn't charboy Pip's business, but it was wizard Conn's. I kept hold of the knapsack. "Are you going to get money for it?" I asked.

His hand shot out and cuffed me on the ear. "Give me the bag, Pip, and no more questions."

All right. I handed over the knapsack.

Sorry, Periwinkle. She wouldn't like losing her stone. I would get it back for her. Sure as sure, I would.

Uproar at magisters meeting this morning. Periwinkle's stone stolen during the night despite precautions. Guard outside her door, stone locked in safe place. Lock picked, apparently, and guard not alerted.

Certain Conn involved. Inspected Peri's room this morning, noticed soot from chimney on floor. Brushed it aside with my foot, assume it was not observed by anyone else.

Am undecided about whether to have a further discussion with Duchess and Underlord about this.

Perhaps not. Will keep my own counsel for now. Must trust that Conn knows what he is doing.

My own locus stone the only one left. Except for Conn's, of course. Means my stone will be the thieves' next target. Must take extra precautions.

CHAPTER 16

I woke up in the cellar of the chimney swifts' house, surrounded by charkids. A lantern was in the middle of the floor, and one of the kids was passing around their dinner from a basket. A swift must've brought it down; the thump of his feet on the stairs had woken me up.

After I'd stolen Periwinkle's

locus magicalicus, Sootle had rowed us back to the Sunrise. I'd only managed to snatch bits of sleep for the past couple of days, so when we arrived at Sootle's house I stumbled down to the cellar and into my blanket. I'd slept the whole day away. My stomach growled.

I sat up with the prickly blanket wrapped around me. Beside me, Pip-cat uncurled itself, got to its four paws, and stretched.

Like me, the charkids were skinny and covered with soot, barefoot and dressed in black. One of the chargirls edged up to me and handed me a hard roll with cheese in it. "What's your name?"

"Pip," I said. "What's yours?"

"Emm," she said. "You Sootle's new charboy?"

I nodded and took a bite of roll-and-cheese.

Another charkid came over, a boy with hair shaved short and eyes rimmed with red, as if he'd been crying. "He's mean, is Sootle," he said.

I shrugged. He wasn't that bad.

"The boss is meaner," said the girl.

The boss? "Sootle's the boss, isn't he?"

"Shhh," whispered the boy, with a quick glance at the ceiling, as if somehow the boss could hear him. He shook his head. "The boss is somebody else."

"Who?" I asked.

Emm glanced toward the ceiling, too. "He's upstairs. In the attic. That's where he stays."

"They keep him in a cage," the boy leaned in to whisper.

A cage?

"'Cos he's so mean," Emm said.

"No, it isn't a cage," another chargirl put in. "It's a room, a metal room."

"Whatever it is, he's out of it now," the boy whispered, "'cos they're having a meeting up there."

A meeting? I got to my feet, swallowing the last bite of my dinner. Maybe at the meeting they'd talk about why the swifts were stealing the locus stones and what they were going to do with them. I started toward the stairs.

The charkids stared. "We're supposed to stay down here," Emm said, grabbing at my ankle. "Drury said so."

I shook her off. "I won't be long," I said.

With Pip following, I went up the stairs and padded through the dark kitchen, then up the even darker stairs, pausing to listen at each door. When I got to the door to the room where I'd first met Sootle, I heard the sound of low talking. I pressed my ear against the keyhole, but couldn't make out the words. Hm. I'd have to take a chance.

Quick as sticks, I cat-footed back down to the kitchen, where I found a scuttle full of kindling, a striker, and a shovel and broom, and lugged it all back to the door. Taking a deep breath and keeping my head down, I went in.

The room was the same as before, blank walls and empty fireplace, and it was chilly. Six chimney swifts and Sootle were sitting around the table. They all stopped talking and looked up as I came in.

"Drury told you charkids to stay in the cellar,"

Sootle said sharply.

I shrugged. "I was asleep." I held up the scuttle. "D'you want a fire?"

Sootle glanced at the empty hearth, then nodded. "Be quick about it, Pip." Then he hunched over the table and spoke in a low voice to the other swifts, and they leaned forward to listen.

I went to the hearth. Since the last time I'd been there and climbed the chimney, somebody had lit a wood fire and let it burn down to ashes. Slowly, keeping my ear on the conversation at the table behind me, I unloaded each piece of wood from the scuttle, then swept up the ashes in the hearth.

The swifts kept talking, but they kept their voices too low for me to hear. They kept somebody in a metal room upstairs? At my side, Pip twitched its prickly cat tail and then climbed up to my shoulder. Hmmm. If I did the seeing-and-hearing spell, Pip's sharp ears would let me hear what the swifts were talking about at the table. I was about to whisper *Tallennar* when the door banged open.

The swifts at the table jumped to their feet. I stayed crouching by the hearth, and peeked over my shoulder to see. Two big men lumbered into the room. My heart gave a sudden jolt of fright. I recognized them. They were the men who'd beaten the fluff out of me at the Heartsease courtyard and then tried to kidnap me. The men stepped aside. A wizard came in the doorway—Nimble, smiling his secret smirk. Nimble? What was *he* doing here?

And then came the boss.

Oh. Oh, no.

The boss was Crowe.

From Duchess Rowan to Underlord Embre

It has been days, and no word from Conn.

Have you heard from Magister Nevery?

The magisters are alarmed, now that Magister Periwinkle's locus stone has been stolen and Nevery's stone is the only one left. They are certain that Conn is responsible, and they grow more impatient. Not as impatient as I am. Why won't he send us a note, at least?

—Rowan J
Dawn Palace
The Sunrise

⊡□◌४ ♀◦◦♀∨⊥ ४◦९ ♤∨◠◠⊡◦⌒
⊼४ ⌐♀◦̈◌⌒⊥◦̈◌∨◦

⊡□◌४ ♀◦◌♀ ४◦९ ◠◌४∨∨ ४◦९◠
∧◦̈⊓◦̈◌ ⊥◌̈ ⊼◦̈ ⊥◦◦̈ ⊡⊼४
४◦९◠⌒◠◦ ◌̈◠⊼◠◠◌̈

Dear Rowan,

You, impatient? Truly, it is hard to imagine such a thing.

No, I haven't heard from Nevery, or from Conn. My man Fist spoke to a potboy at a tavern who said a blue-eyed, black-haired gutterboy with a strange cat was there several days ago. But the potboy would say nothing about what the gutterboy wanted at the tavern. Can we assume the "cat" was Conn's dragon and that Conn wasn't at the tavern to drink red-streak gin?

I think we must trust Conn to know his business and leave him to it.

Yours always,

Embre

Dusk House

The Twilight

Crowe, here in the city. My stomach clenched with icy fear. *He* had sent the minions to kidnap me. He was behind the locus stone thefts. The anstriker spell had gone wrong somehow, and he'd been here all along. I *had* to get away before he saw me.

Crowe stepped smoothly past his minions, past Nimble, his cold gaze probing the room.

I kept my head down. Let him not see me. Please don't see me.

His gaze swept right past me at the hearth and came to rest on Sootle. "I see you've started without me," he said.

His voice was just like I remembered from when I was a scared little kid. Flat, quiet. He made the room feel colder just by stepping into it. I risked a quick glance. He looked just the same. Middling height, not very big, not very old. Neat black suit and neatly combed and oiled black hair. He didn't *look* noticeable, but everyone in the room knew he was there. As if he took up a lot more space than most people.

Maybe he wouldn't see me at all. If I stayed crouched and quiet and looked like a charboy sweeping out a hearth. My hands shaking, I swept up a bit more of the ash from the fireplace and put it into the scuttle.

"We were just talking, sir," Sootle said, stepping quickly aside from the head of the table.

"So I see," Crowe said. He moved to the table and stood there. He had his back to me, but I knew Crowe, I knew he was aware of everything and everyone in the room. He crooked a finger and his minions stepped up beside him. Crowe whispered something. The minions nodded and went to stand in front of the door, burly arms folded across their chests. Nimble stood next to the table, still wearing his smirk; he'd glanced around the room, but he hadn't recognized me, I didn't think. Moving carefully, I got some soot from the hearth I was sweeping and rubbed it over my face. Not much of a disguise, really.

Sootle lifted the knapsack from under his chair and pulled out one of the rag-wrapped packages. "Here it is, sir," he said, setting it on the table.

"Ah." Crowe unwrapped the package. The tourmalifine cage with Periwinkle's locus magicalicus in it. The wires of the cage glinted silvery green in the room's dim light. "Very good," Crowe said, handing the cage to Nimble, who stowed it in a pocket of his wizard's robe. Crowe glanced at the minions at the door and nodded. Then Crowe turned away from the table and said something to Sootle in a low voice. Sootle nodded.

I edged deeper into the shadows by the hearth. Pip-cat crouched on my shoulder as if it was ready to leap on somebody. I kept my head down. My breath came fast and my hands were shaking. I clenched them into fists to make them stop.

Crowe's footsteps sounded loud in the quiet room. They came around the table. *Step, step, step.*

Keep going. Walk past me, just walk past.

The footsteps stopped in front of me. Black leather shoes, black trousers. A hand reached out, grabbed my arm, and jerked me to my feet, and then I felt his cold fingers under my chin, lifting my head so he could see my face. His pale eyes looked me up and down. His minions loomed up behind him.

"It is a good disguise, Connwaer," Crowe said in his cold, flat voice. "But as you grow up you look more and more like your mother." He smudged his thumb across my cheek. "And the soot can't hide that from me."

I stepped out of his reach, my back against the fireplace. Pip, on my shoulder, snarled, and its cat tail bristled.

"Take him," Crowe said over his shoulder to the minions.

As the minions' big hands reached for me, I squirmed sideways. If I could just get to the door—

The minion came after me. I shouted the dazzler spell. The magic worked perfectly—a gust of sparks exploded from Pip's mouth and whirled into the minion's eyes; he flinched away and threw up his arm to block the light. The sparks buzzed around him like angry bees. The chimney swifts were shouting and running to block the door. The other minion lunged after me.

"*Anafinaloth!*" I shouted, the dazzler spell again. Pip leaped up, and a bolt of light shot into Crowe's eyes.

"Shut him up!" Crowe said, backing away, his

eyes streaming. "Don't let him use the magic!"

The other minion leaped for me. He grabbed the front of my sweater and slammed me against the wall, and I gasped out the needle-prickler spell; he shrieked and let me go, slapping at his arms and legs as if he was being stung all over by wasps. I scrambled away from him and headed for the door.

Nimble, gripping his locus stone, blocked my way. Two swifts loomed up beside him.

Not that way, then.

As the swifts reached for me, I scrambled under the table, dodging reaching arms, and came out next to the hearth.

"Come on, Pip," I gasped, and, kicking firewood out of the way, darted to the chimney. Swifts tried grabbing my legs, but I was too quick for them, climbing up the narrow chimney. Pip climbed after me, its cat paws clinging to the bricks. At the top, I stuck my head out and felt the cold air of night and saw the lights of the city and the dark sky overhead. Quickly I climbed out of the chimney and raced across the roof, Pip bounding after me. I got to the edge of the roof. A dark alleyway lay below, and then the roof of the house next door. A long way to jump, but not too far. From below, I heard the front door of Sootle's house bang open, and a chimney swift's shout.

Taking a deep breath, I jumped, landing with a splat on the slate rooftiles. I listened for a second, and didn't hear a shout from below. On stealthy feet, I padded across to the next house and made the alley jump again.

When I'd been a thief, it had been easy to get into houses to steal things. I'd just find a gutter drain that led up to the roof, and then I'd climb in a high window, because often enough people left them unlocked. Soon I came to a house with a gutter drain, and shimmied down it to the ground. With the cobblestones cold under my feet and the sound of shouts and pounding feet behind me, Pip and I fled into the night.

Crowe, Crowe, Crowe, I kept thinking. Crowe here, in the city. Crowe after me. The thought made me run faster. I couldn't let him catch me.

With Pip-cat bounding after me, I rounded a corner, my bare feet silent on the cobblestoned street. I ducked into a dark alleyway. Leaning against a brick wall, panting, I closed my eyes; the sound of chasing footsteps faded. Pip crawled up the wall beside me and clung to the bricks over my head.

I edged to the corner and peered around. Pip leaped from the wall onto my shoulder and poked its whiskery cat nose around the corner, too. A few werelight streetlamps glowed, but the houses and shops along the street were dark. All was quiet.

Grrrr, Pip growled.

I slipped back into the alley and slid down the wall to sit on the cold cobbles. "Come here, Pip," I whispered. Pip hopped onto my knees and fluffed its tail. Time to turn it back into a dragon. Putting my hand on the prickly place between the cat-Pip's ears, I whispered the reverse-embirrimer spell. As the spell flashed, I shoved Pip under my black sweater so the sparks and white-bright light wouldn't show every minion in the Sunrise where we were hiding.

I hunched over as the light flared out.

Pip squirmed. I lifted my sweater, and dragon-Pip crawled out, sneezing sparks and rubbing at its snout with its claw-paw.

"All right?" I whispered.

It cocked its head and gave me a glary look with its ember-red eye.

Step-clatter-step, I heard, the sound of running feet. I snuck a look 'round the corner. Chimney swifts, racing down the middle of the cobbled street, coming straight toward my hiding place. A hooded, cloaked figure glided along a few steps behind them. One of the swifts pointed. I ducked back into the dark alley, and with Pip swooping after me on its golden wings, skiffed away. I took a couple of quick turns until the sound of chasing footsteps faded.

I caught my breath. Now what?

It is not a bad thing to ask for help now and then, Nevery had said.

Right. He was right. I couldn't fight Crowe alone. It was time to find help.

I headed for home.

CHAPTER 18

As I crept up the dark street toward the Night Bridge, I kept my ears and eyes open, but didn't see anything that made me jumpy.

But they were there, waiting in the shadows. Two soot-smudged chimney swifts, who stepped out into the road as I started across the bridge. One of them shouted over his shoulder, and two more swifts emerged from the darkness.

They chased. I ran. Pip flew.

'Round a corner, down a narrow alley, through a park, then down another street, 'til I'd gotten away from them.

So they'd blocked the bridge. Of course they had. Crowe wasn't stupid; he knew I'd head for Heartsease. Right. I was on the Sunrise side of the city, so the best place to try next would be the Dawn Palace. Coming in the middle of the night and looking like a charboy, I might have trouble getting to see Rowan, but sure as sure the guards would take me to see Captain Kerrn.

That decided, I headed up the hill.

As I rounded a corner, there they were again, two swifts and a minion. Catching sight of me, they chased me back down the hill. I ran silent as a shadow and gave them the slip, and fetched up on the riverbank, panting, with Pip flapping behind me, also panting.

A boat. They'd blocked the bridge, so I needed a boat.

In the distance I heard a shout, then running footsteps.

Drats! They were coming again.

Quick as sticks, I skiffed down stone steps to a dock, and I was in luck. A rowboat with oars set inside. I untied the rope and jumped into the boat; Pip jumped in after me and I shoved us off the dock. Heavy feet pounded down the steps, but we were away.

I rowed hard, thinking even harder. Sure as sure, Crowe's minions would be waiting to jump me if I went to Heartsease, just like they'd jumped me once before. So I wouldn't go there, I'd go to ground in the Twilight and make my way to Embre at Dusk House. Crowe would never catch me in the twisty streets of the Twilight; he never had before, anyway.

I beached the boat on a stretch of mud near a Twilight warehouse that loomed like a cliff face out of the dark, then climbed up to a rutted path. With Pip flying behind me, I skiffed along until I got to Ten Crane Street that ran along the river.

From down the street, shouts and a flare of light.

Curse it, they'd gotten ahead of me again!

I whirled and headed back the way I'd come. All right, all right. The back alleys. It'd take longer, but I could get to Dusk House that way. I started down another alley and heard running footsteps coming, so I headed in the other direction. 'Round another corner and across a wider street; I tripped on a pothole and went sprawling. Pip sprawled in a puddle beside me. Scrambling to my feet, I paused to grab up panting Pip, and raced away again.

Rounding a corner, I caught a quick-look behind me at the chasers. Swifts again, with that same hooded figure as before. A wizard. Nimble?

My legs quivered with tiredness as I pelted down one alley and up another. Rest. I needed a rest. I slipped into a narrow gap between two falling-down houses and ducked behind a pile of trash to catch my breath. Pip climbed up to my shoulder and clung there, its tail limp, its head drooping.

"Tired?" I whispered to it.

Krrrr, Pip breathed.

At the end of the alley, a flare of light. "He's down this way!" Nimble's whiny voice shouted.

Curse it! I jumped to my feet. It was almost like they were tracking me!

Wait. How could I have been so stupid? They *were* tracking me. Nimble had his locus stone—he was working with Crowe, so he must have lied about it being stolen—and he must have a scrying globe, too. He was using the anstriker spell.

I stumble-ran through the gap between the houses and right into the arms of two swifts.

"Finalelenon!" I shouted, the needle-prickler spell, and they shrieked as tiny spell-sparks stung them all over. I jerked myself out of their hands and ran.

Right, so Crowe would have his minions and swifts spread like a net all over the city, searching for me, tracking me. Time to do something he wouldn't expect.

I headed for the mudflats.

I stumbled up to the mudlarks' shack. A wind had started blowing and a couple of drops of rain pattered down. Thunder grumbled in the lands beyond the Sunrise.

Way behind me, at the head of the path along the mudflats, was a glimmer of lights. Followers. They were coming.

Bang-bang-bang on the door, and I leaned my head against the doorframe, gasping for breath. Come *on*.

The door creaked open.

"*Lothfalas*," I panted, and Pip breathed out a glowing cloud of sparks that hovered over our heads. The light showed the mudlark Den in his warm coat and, peering over his shoulder, the girl Jo. In the shadows behind them, I saw the gleaming eyes of the mudlark-kids, sitting up in their blankets.

"What d'you want?" Den grunted.

I caught my breath. "I need your help."

"Helped you once already," Den said. "Now take yourself off." He started to close the door.

Jo pushed past him. "No—wait," she said. She looked from my face to Pip on my shoulder. "I know who you really are. You did magic there, with the light. You're that wizard boy. We heard a story about you." She nudged Den. "Remember?"

Den shrugged. "Maybe."

Jo went on. "You're the one who was a gutterkid, like us, and blew up that other wizard's house and almost got hanged for it, and stole a magical jewel from the Underlord. That's you, right?"

Not exactly, but it was too much to explain. "Right," I said. I glanced back toward the city. The followers were closer, their lights bobbing up and down as they ran along the path. The rain pattered down harder.

"Yeah, I remember," Den said. "The gutter-boy-wizard. They coming for you?" Den wiped raindrops off his face.

Oh, he wasn't going to like this. "It's Crowe. He's come back to Wellmet."

"Crowe?" Den repeated. Beside him, Jo went pale. "And you led him *here*?" Den turned to speak to the other mudlarks. "Get up. We're leaving." Behind him, the kids were gathering their rags and blankets.

"Sorry," I said. Drats, I should have thought of this. "I'll lead them away if I can." I talked faster. "But I need you to take a message for me. Will you help me?"

Den opened his mouth—to say *no*, sure as sure—but Jo interrupted. Maybe she was the boss, after all. "He's a gutterkid like us, Den, even if he is a wizard," she said. "And it's Crowe he's talking about. Crowe's bad." She spoke to me. "We don't want him back here, sending his minions to beat us up if we don't give him most of our takings. We'll help. We'd better hurry." She pointed at the mud-flats path. "They're getting close."

"All right," Den said to me. "What d'you need?"

In the distance I heard a shout. The lights moved closer. Torches.

"Will you take a message to the wizard Nevery, on Heartsease island?"

"To a wizard?" Den stared at me. Raindrops

pattered down around us. Jo nudged him, and he shrugged. "Got to get them settled first." He pointed over his shoulder toward the other mud-larks. "But once that's done I'll find this Nevery. What message?"

I steadied Pip on my shoulder and got ready to run. "Tell him it's Crowe who's stealing the locus stones."

"Crowe stealing the stones," Den repeated. "Right. What else?"

"Tell Nevery that Nimble's one of them, and if he doesn't hear from me soon he should use the anstriker spell to find me, and to look for Crowe." What else? "Tell him Crowe's using a house in the Sunrise, along the river."

Jo pulled at Den's sleeve. "Come on."

I took a few steps away, then turned back. "Tell Nevery to be careful," I added. "And I'll help you later if I can."

"Sure you will," Den said. "Come on," he said to the mudlarks, who had crept outside. They faded away into the rainy darkness beyond the shack.

I led the minions and swifts on a chase through the marshes and mud. Then, too tired to run any more, I hid.

CHAPTER 19

I crouched behind a clump of rattly dry grasses at the edge of the mudflats, panting, my heart pounding. Pip huddled at my feet. The minions and swifts surrounded us.

"Come on out, wizard boy," one of the chimney swifts growled.

Not likely. The circle closed in. Trying to make a last run for it, I jumped up, shouting the dazzler spell, but some-body seized me from behind and clamped a hand over my mouth, and then the swift Drury was there, gripping my muddy legs, lifting me off the ground. I squirmed and thrashed. Pip launched itself at Drury's face, hissing and clawing, but he ducked his head and held me tight. Then one of the minions, his eyes streaming from the dazzler spell, grabbed Pip by the scruff of its neck and stuffed it into a sack. Sootle brought another sack, one damp with the rain, and he and Drury shoved me into it. I shouted part of the needle-prickler spell and some-body thumped me, a punch right in my stomach that took my breath away.

"Quickly," I heard Nimble's voice say. "He's waiting by the river."

He. Crowe, he meant. I tried squirm-worming my way out of the bag, but somebody picked me up and threw me over his shoulder, and off we went, squelching along the mudflat path.

As we went bump-bump-bumping along, I

caught my breath and, as loud as I could, shouted the needle-prickler spell. A couple of paces away, I heard Nimble shriek and drop the bag that Pip was in. It landed with a squelchy thud on the ground.

Then—*thump*—and ow, another breathtaking punch. "Stay quiet in there," growled the minion carrying me. "No more spells."

He jogged along for couple of long minutes, went over some rough ground, then paused.

"In here," one of the chimney swifts said. "Hurry."

The minion tossed me and I bounced off what felt like a wall and crashed onto the ground. Catching my breath, I pulled the damp sack off my head. The surface under me felt bumpy and cold. Light from the torches flickered off wire mesh. I reached out with my hands and touched more wires.

Had they put me into a cage?

I shook my head. Something was wrong. Usually I could feel the steady strength of Arhionvar and the warmth of the old Wellmet magic, but they had disappeared. I couldn't feel my locus magicalicus, either. My head felt echoing and empty. "Pip!" I shouted.

"Quiet," a swift said, and thumped the cage. Other minions and swifts were moving, dark shadows beyond the light of the torch.

"Get the cloth," Sootle said. Rain dripped from the ends of his stringy black hair. Drury nodded and went down the bank to what looked like a rowboat beached on the muddy shore; he returned with a folded canvas and rope. With the rain still pelting down, they wrapped the cage in the canvas.

Inside the cage was dark, and the sound of the raindrops was a muffled *pattery-pat* on the cloth over my head. The cage was box-shaped, made of metal mesh, big enough that I could lie down in it if I curled up, and a little taller than I was. I used my damp sweater-sleeve to wipe the rain off my face. Without the magics, I felt cold and alone. Shivering, I crouched at the bottom of the cage.

I wasn't dead, at least. If they wanted me dead,

they'd have done it already. So they wanted me for something else.

After a moment I heard the sound of footsteps and low voices, talking.

"Put it in," I heard Crowe's cold voice say. A prickle of icy dread ran over my skin. So he was here, too.

A swift said something, and Crowe answered. "Yes, the other house. Hurry."

The cage lifted and jounced along and was set down, right-side-up. The ground rocked. The rowboat, then. It rocked again, people stepping into the boat, and the slither of ropes as they tied the cage down, then a push and we were out in the river.

No, they were not going to take me that easily.

If I rocked the boat, they'd have to go back to shore. I got to my feet and hurled myself against the side of the cage. The boat rocked. I threw myself back against the other side and the boat rocked again. I heard splashing and a curse, and then a *thwack* that shook the cage, somebody hitting it with an oar, I guessed.

"Stop that," hissed Sootle's voice, and then another *thwack*.

Instead of stopping, I flung myself against the side of the cage again. The boat lurched and I heard more cursing and the sound of river water slopping over the sides of the boat.

"Stop," Crowe's sharp voice ordered. "Unwrap it."

A few jerks and tugs, and the canvas was off the cage. I crouched at the bottom of it, water sloshing around my bare feet. Rain pelted down from overhead. I was in the middle of the rowboat, Sootle at the oars just behind me, Nimble in the front, with a tangle of rope and the sack with Pip in it at his feet, along with a werelight lantern.

Crowe sat on a wide plank seat. He wore a dark cloak, and in the dim light his eyes gleamed like silver locks with dark keyholes. Raindrops streamed down his face. He leaned toward me. "You'd like to go for a swim, Connwaer?" he whispered. He nodded at Sootle and pointed at my cage. "Put him in."

"Yes sir," Sootle said. He set aside the oars, swiped the stringy hair out of his eyes, and he and a nastily smiling Nimble gripped the cage and heaved it over the side of the boat, into the river.

Water flooded in, icy cold, over my legs, up to my neck. I gripped the top of the cage with my fingers, holding my head above the waves, gasping from the cold. I peered up through the darkness, through the lashing rain and the hair dripping into my eyes, at Crowe looking down at me from the edge of the boat, at Nimble and Sootle holding the sides of the cage.

"Lower," Crowe said.

Down the cage went. I caught one quick gasp of air and the icy-cold water closed over my head. Everything went quiet except for the bump of the cage against the side of the boat and the faint hiss of rain hitting the surface of the river.

The cage came up. Water streamed from the wire mesh. I caught my breath.

Crowe's face leaned down toward me. "So you wanted to upset the boat, did you?" he asked. "It follows that you must like water. D'you want some more?"

A wave sloshed over my face. I swallowed murk-muddy river water and coughed it out again. I shook my head. No, I didn't want any more.

"Are you going to cooperate with me?" Crowe asked.

Oh, drats. "No," I croaked out.

Crowe's face set, and he jerked a nod at Sootle and Nimble. "Down."

They lowered the cage and the water closed over my head. My hair floated in front of my eyes like riverweed. I clung to the wires at the top of the cage, my fingers numb with cold, staring up through the murky water but seeing only darkness. The water squeezed at my lungs, wanting me to breathe it in. Thunder roared in my ears and the blackness pressed in around me.

My fingers loosened their grip on the wires.
Let me up!

CHAPTER 20

Just as the last bubble of air in my lungs was popping, the cage lurched up.

I dragged in a choking breath, then another one, as Nimble and Sootle hauled the cage back into the boat. I coughed, my black sweater heavy with water, my hair dripping down into my eyes. Usually I'd have the magic to draw on for help. This time, I was alone.

I looked up, shivering.

Crowe stared down at me from his seat in the boat. He put his hand into his pocket and pulled something out. The clicker-ticker, his calculating device. *Click* it went as he turned one of the bone disks. *Click-tick-tick.*

"You were under the water for forty counts," Crowe said, in his dead-flat voice. "I don't think you can last for much longer than that, but we can try it and see. Will you come quietly now, Connwaer?"

As an answer, I dragged myself up, my legs shaking, and flung myself against the side of the cage. The boat tipped.

Crowe grasped the edge of the boat to balance himself. His face turned bone white. He narrowed his eyes. "Put him in again," he ordered.

Nimble grabbed the edge of the cage. The swift Sootle hesitated. "It'll be dawn soon, sir. We need to get off the river."

Crowe frowned. "Yes. We do," he said after a moment.

"Right, sir," Sootle said. "We can have him out of there and give him a quick knock on the head." He pointed at me. "He'd come along quietly then, wouldn't he?"

"No," Crowe said. "No knocks on the head. I need him functionable, for now." He studied me. *Click-tick*. I could almost see the gears turning in his mind. "The dragon," he said. "Give it to me."

Nimble handed him the squirming sack with Pip in it. Crowe held it over the side of the boat, over the deep-dark water. His cold eyes watched me. Slowly he lowered the sack until it rested on the top of the water; then, leaning over, he shoved it under the surface.

I gripped the wire mesh of the cage, straining to see. "Pip!" I shouted. Under the water, the bag bumped and bulged, as if Pip was thrashing around, trying to escape. "Stop," I gasped. "Let it up! I'll come without a fuss, all right?"

Crowe studied me for a moment longer, waited a few heartbeats more, then he heaved the dripping sack from the water. He tossed it on the bottom of the boat; it landed with a soggy thud.

Pip? In the dim light, I saw the sack twitch. I let out a breath of relief. Pip was still alive in there.

"Interesting," Crowe said. "Very"—*click-tick*—"interesting."

I did as I'd promised, didn't make a fuss as they wrapped up the cage again and rowed across the river. It was a quick trip. The boat bumped up against a dock, and Nimble and Sootle lifted the cage out and carried it up some steps and then into a house. A different house? They hadn't walked enough steps for it to be the same house in the Sunrise they'd used before. Where were we?

Bump-thump and up stairs and more stairs, and the cage was set down with a thud and the canvas covering was taken off.

One of the chimney swifts brought a lantern into the room, set it on a table, and went out. Except for me in my cage, the room was empty. Outside the door, I heard voices, people talking.

I got to my feet and looked around. The cage was made of wire mesh that glinted green in the lanternlight. Tourmalifine? Just like the little box they'd put Periwinkle's locus stone into. Under my bare feet, the wires felt cold. I stepped to the side and pressed my fingers against the mesh, and the cold from the wires seeped into them. I shivered in my soggy sweater and clothes and coughed a bit more of the river out of my lungs.

The cage stood in the middle of a big room. An attic, I realized, the top floor of a house. The walls were whitewashed and the floor uncarpeted wood. On one side the ceiling sloped down to meet the wall, which had a row of small windows in it. The sky outside was just turning the gray of early morning. A few paces away from my cage was the table where the swift had set the lantern, and on the table was another cage, just like mine but a lot smaller. Pip had been stuffed into it. The wires pressed up against its scaly sides, and where they touched sparks snapped, making Pip growl and cringe away.

Oh. Tourmalifine wires. Pip's scales were made of slowsilver. According to the treatise I'd read about pyrotechnics, tourmalifine and slowsilver were contrafusives, and that meant—

—the cage was hurting Pip.

"Pip," I whispered. The dragon snarled and bit at the wires. Sparks flashed.

The door to the attic swung open. Crowe walked in with Nimble, followed by two chimney swifts, Drury and Sootle.

"—and then we'll deal with the duchess's guards," Crowe was saying to Nimble, who nodded. The swifts waited by the door. Ignoring Pip, Crowe and Nimble came to stand before my cage.

Crowe looked me up and down. He put his hand into his pocket. *Click-tick*, I heard. *Click-tick-tick-tick*. "So," he said in his cold, blank voice. "You've delivered yourself into my hands. Not very clever of you, was it, allowing yourself to be captured?"

He was right. I was stupid. But not as stupid as

he was for returning to Wellmet. "Why'd you come back?" I asked.

Crowe's eyes narrowed. The old me wouldn't have asked that question. He would've stayed quiet, the frightened kid who'd run away from Crowe and his minions to hide in the Twilight. Maybe Crowe still saw a poor street kid when he looked at me, but this Conn was a wizard, not just a gutterboy.

Crowe paused for a moment, calculating his answer. "Why did I come out of exile? Because my associate Nimble wrote me a letter. He told me that Wellmet was being run by children." His lip curled into a sneer. "A child duchess and a child Underlord. I had to come back and see for myself."

Oh.

"And I found it was true," he went on. "Not only that, they'd appointed a boy wizard to be the ducal magister. I realized that after the hard times it has faced, Wellmet needs someone older and steadier to control it. Somebody with more experience."

"You?" I asked.

"Who better to seize such a moment?" Crowe

said. He gave a dry smile. "I sent my men to bring you in. You managed to evade me, and my plans were put into disarray. And yet now you put yourself into my hands. Thanks to you, Nephew, I am almost ready."

Ready for what?

He gazed at me for a moment. "Almost," he said quietly, "ready." He reached out and tapped the wire mesh. I edged away from him until I was pressed into the corner of the cage. "You are going to work for me."

No. I wasn't. I shook my head.

Crowe glanced at the table where Pip was squirming inside its cage. Then he looked back at me with his cold eyes. *Click-tick-tick* went the calculating device in his pocket. "I'll ask again later and see what you have to say then."

"You can ask again if you want," I said. "I'll never work for you." *Never.*

Crowe fixed me with a cold glare.

Then Nimble leaned over and spoke quietly to him. "We've got to get you hidden away again," he said.

"My room has been made ready?" Crowe asked, turning toward the door.

"Yes," Nimble answered, with a side-smirk at me. "Just downstairs." Crowe and Nimble stepped out the door, taking the swifts with them.

The attic room was dim, lit only by the early morning light peeking in the windows and the flashes of sparks from Pip's cage. I heard the dragon snapping and growling, but after a while its snarls turned to a low keening sound. It sounded hurt.

I had to get Pip out of there. With my fingers, I examined every corner of my cage but couldn't feel a door or a lock, no weak spots. The wires radiated cold. Shivering, I curled up in a corner and tried to think.

Crowe had a room waiting for him, he'd said. But the charkids had said Crowe had been kept in a cage, hadn't they? No, a metal room, they'd said. Why?

My cage was made of tourmalifine wire. Tourmalifine repelled magic.

Right.

I'd escried for Crowe and the anstriker spell had said he wasn't here, but clear as clear, Crowe had been in Wellmet all along. Crowe must have a small room made of tourmalifine wires, and he went inside it to hide himself from any wizard who might be searching for him.

Very clever.

That meant while I was in the cage I was hidden from the magics, too. If Nevery tried the anstriker spell to look for me, as I'd told the mudlarks to tell him to do, he wouldn't see me. He was worried about me already, and he'd get even more worried if I disappeared.

I put my head down on my knees and shivered, and listened to Pip keening in its cage. I felt empty, the separation from the magics and from Pip like a gaping hole inside me. After a while the sky outside the row of windows brightened and the light of day crept into the room.

From the rest of the house came muffled

bumpings and thumpings, and low murmurings, as if it was full of people getting ready to do something and trying to be quiet about it. Where was the house? I wondered. And what was Crowe up to? He planned to take over the city, that was clear, but he was being stupid if he thought he'd succeed. Rowan had Captain Kerrn and the palace guards, and Embre had his men, and Nevery was the most powerful wizard in the city and still had his locus stone. What did Crowe have? A set of magisters' locus stones that he couldn't even use, Nimble, and a gang of chimney swifts? Not enough for his plans, I'd bet.

After a long time, hours I guessed, the door to the attic swung open. I got stiffly to my feet. Two swifts came in. Sootle carried a tray with a bowl and a mug on it. The other swift stayed by the door.

Sootle brought the tray up to my cage. "Food," he said, and set the tray on the floor. "Don't give me any trouble."

Sure as sure I'd give him trouble, if I could.

"Back off," he said, and pointed to the other side of the cage.

I backed off.

He pulled a thumbnail-sized gray stone from his pocket. A keystone. It had magic in it, for opening locks, even for people who weren't wizards. He touched the stone to the side of the cage and it opened, like a door. With his foot, he shoved the tray into the cage.

I threw myself across the cage, trying to get out the door, but he was ready for me.

"None of that," he said sharply, and shoved me back, slamming the cage door closed again.

Curse it.

Crouching, I looked up at Sootle, who stared down at me, scowling. Crowe's man. "What d'you get out of this," I asked, "helping him?"

"Shut up," Sootle answered.

"I'm just curious," I said. "He must've promised you something."

Sootle folded his arms and nodded. "He'll be

the power of this city."

Well, the real power of Wellmet was the magics, but they weren't like people. They were huge and the city was theirs, in a way, but they didn't want to rule, like Crowe did. I didn't expect Sootle to understand that, though.

"Don't bother saying Crowe's promise don't mean anything," Sootle said. "We swifts will hold him to it."

It didn't sound much like they trusted each other. "What promise?" I pushed.

"Crowe takes over, we swifts become his right-hand people. Minions, like those others he brought in, running the city. We'll be living up in the Dawn Palace like fine ladies and gentlemen."

"It's not as fine up there as you think," I told him.

"Shut up," Sootle repeated, and went to stand by the door.

I sat on the cage floor and ate the food he'd brought, cold tea, a couple of pieces of cold toast with jam that I'd stepped on when trying to get out, and a bowl of cold porridge with an egg on it. I gulped it down, wishing I could share the egg with Pip, as I'd done the day before.

I was drinking down the tea when Crowe walked in. The swifts, who'd been lounging against the wall while I ate, straightened and fell in behind him.

The food turned into a heavy stone in my stomach. I swallowed to keep it there, where it belonged. I hadn't changed my mind. I wasn't going to work for Crowe, no matter what he said.

Crowe paused at the table and examined Pip, then came to stand before my cage. "Your dragon doesn't look very well, Connwaer," he said in his cold voice.

I didn't answer. I could beg him to let Pip out, but he wouldn't. Unless it worked into his plans somehow.

The swift Sootle had put on heavy gloves. He picked up Pip's cage and carried it closer, and put it up against my cage.

"Pip," I whispered, and reached through the wire mesh and brushed its scales with my fingertips. Pip shivered and cracked its eyes open, then gave a low *krrrr*.

Sootle jerked the cage away.

"Are you going to work for me?" Crowe asked.

What? "No," I answered. Of course not.

Crowe bent and stared straight into my eyes. "I will kill the dragon," he said.

Sootle pulled out a long, thin knife and held it up to Pip's cage.

My heart gave a sudden jolt of dread and fright. I gripped the wire mesh. "No!"

Crowe nodded at the swift, and he shook Pip's cage. Sparks flared and Pip thrashed, making a high, keening sound. "I will kill it," Crowe said again.

He would. I tore my eyes away from Pip. "Please, please don't. Don't hurt it."

"You will work for me," Crowe said.

Yes, anything. I'd do anything. I nodded.

"You do this job for me and I will spare the life of your dragon. You agree?"

"Yes," I said. My voice sounded choked, and I realized I was crying. I rubbed the tears off my cheeks and took a shaky breath. Yes. I'd work for Crowe if it meant saving Pip's life. He'd calculated that right.

"I thought you'd change your mind, Connwaer," Crowe said. He turned and spoke to the other swift. "Get a pencil and paper." The swift nodded and left the room.

Crowe examined me with his pale eyes. "First, Connwaer, you are going to write a note."

No word from Conn for a few days. Then, on way home from meeting with duchess at Dawn Palace, sooty child dressed all in black thrust a note into my hand, ran away.

To Nevery,
Please meet me tonight at the chophouse on Strangle Street.
    From Connwaer

Strange note. Will meet him, of course. He had better tell me what is going on.

CHAPTER 21

Crowe's chimney swifts blindfolded me and led me out of the
place they'd brought me and
rowed me across the river to the dim-
dark, damp Twilight. They took off the
blindfold and stayed right on my heels
as I left the dockyards and warehouses
and climbed the steep streets.

I paused in the alley across from
the chophouse on Strangle Street. It

was good to be out of the cage, feeling the magics around me again. They were still settled in their places, but they both felt . . . prickly. Uneasy. I couldn't do anything about it, now.

"This it?" the swift Sootle asked. He carried a knapsack.

I didn't answer.

My men will go with you, Crowe had said. *They will be listening, and they will know if you give the wizard some kind of signal. Get in, do the job, and get out. The dragon pays for any misstep on your part. Understand?*

I understood. I wouldn't try anything. I would do the job and I would go straight back to the house, back to Pip.

Still, Crowe hadn't won yet. If the mudlarks had delivered my message to Nevery, he'd know something was wrong, that I'd written the note asking him to meet me here because Crowe had his hooks in me. He'd be careful.

But if the mudlark Den hadn't delivered the

message yet, Nevery'd be walking right into a trap.

Across the street, the windows of the chophouse glowed dimly. The cobblestones gleamed, wet with the day's rain. Fog lingered along the edges of the falling-down buildings. My sweater was still damp from my dunking in the river, and I shivered. Nevery might wait for me in the chophouse for a long time.

The chophouse door swung open. Somebody stepped out into the street.

"That him?" whispered the swift named Drury, who loomed beside me.

I shook my head.

After a while, a group of factory workers coming late off a shift trooped past. They didn't see us where we lurked in our dark alleyway. The street fell quiet again.

At last, the dim light in the chophouse went out. The door swung open and a dark figure stepped out.

Nevery.

He paused and adjusted his hat, then, without a

backward glance, set off toward the river, his cane going *tap, tap* against the cobblestones.

Taking a shaky breath, I left the shadows of the alley and went after Nevery on feather-light feet, following him down the dark, steep street.

One thing a good pickpocket learns is *tells*, which is when people tell where they're keeping something valuable. They don't mean to tell, but they almost always do something to give it away.

Nevery usually kept his locus magicalicus in his cloak pocket, but when he'd stepped out the chophouse door, I'd seen his tell—he checked the breast pocket of his suit coat, patting it with his hand before he went on. He probably thought he'd put it there for safekeeping.

It wasn't safe from me, though.

As he turned off of Strangle Street, I darted up beside him, no more than a shadow in the night, dipped into his suit pocket and—*quick hands*—snatched up his locus magicalicus.

He missed it at once and whirled, his cloak

swirling around him.

I ducked away, but not fast enough. He saw me. *Sorry, Nevery. Sorry.*

"Connwaer!" he shouted, and I was gone, melting into the shadows.

I heard the *step step tap* of him coming after me, and then I slipped into the alley where Sootle waited with his knapsack. He pulled out the tiny tourmalifine cage and I dropped the locus magicalicus into it. He snapped it closed. There. Nevery wouldn't be able to sense where it was. To him, the stone had just disappeared.

My eyes blindfolded again, I climbed the stairs with a swift ahead of me and one just behind with his hand on my shoulder. They marched me up to the attic and took off the blindfold.

"Back in the cage," Drury said, giving me a push.

Not yet. I stumbled to the table and bent to look into Pip's cage. The little dragon lay on its side, panting a little. Its scales had turned dusty-dull. "Will you put it in with me?" I asked. Pip might do better if its slowsilver scales weren't touching the tourmalifine wires.

The room's door opened and Crowe came in. He saw me. "Put him back in the cage," he said sharply.

Sootle touched a keystone to the side of the big cage and it swung open. Drury grabbed me by the scruff and shoved me inside. He closed the door behind me, sealing the cage, shutting me away from the magics again.

Crowe came farther into the room. "You have it?" he asked.

"Yes, sir," Sootle said, and pulled the tiny tourmalifine cage from the knapsack.

Nevery's locus magicalicus lay inside, a small stone so dark it was like a bit of swirling night against the glimmering green wires.

Crowe turned the box, examining the stone inside, and then set it on the table. "Good," he said. "Now for the last magister's locus stone."

For once, Crowe had counted wrong. "You've

got Nevery's," I said. "That's all of them."

"No it isn't," Crowe said, his voice cold and quiet. "There is one more. You're a magister too, Nephew. The ducal magister. Had you forgotten?"

What? "But my locus stone is in Pip."

"Yes," Crowe said. "That is a well-known fact." He turned away from my cage and spoke to the swift. "Take the dragon out."

Sootle took a pair of leather gloves from his coat pocket and put them on. Then he touched the keystone to the side of Pip's cage and it opened, and he reached in and pulled Pip out. Pip shivered, but didn't fight. The dragon looked very small in Sootle's gloved hands.

"Do it," Crowe ordered.

With a quick glance at me, Sootle reached into his pocket and pulled out the long, thin-bladed knife.

What? "But I did the job!" I gasped out. "You said you wouldn't hurt Pip."

"So I did." Crowe turned away. "Get on with it,"

he ordered. "Cut the locus stone out of the dragon."

Pip! I flung myself against the wire mesh and the cage rocked. *No, no, no!*

Frowning, Sootle brought the knife up to Pip's chest and glanced at Crowe, who nodded.

A quick thrust, and the knife plunged into Pip, right up to the hilt. My own heart shuddered and shattered into a thousand pieces.

In the swift's hands, Pip twitched and went limp. Sootle let go and Pip's body tumbled to the floor.

CHAPTER 22

I crouched with my forehead pushed up against the cold wires of my cage.

Pip's body lay crumpled on the floor, just beyond the reach of my fingers. It lay on its side, one wing crushed beneath it, the knife hilt sticking out of its chest. In a moment, Sootle would come and cut my locus stone out of Pip's body so Crowe

could use it for whatever he was planning.

Crowe, his back to me, was talking to the swifts, giving them more orders, but the words didn't make sense, they just sounded like a roaring in my ears. I felt stiff and heavy and numb. I'd been stupid. I should've known better than to steal Nevery's locus stone for Crowe. And now Pip was dead. *Dead.*

Pip's body shivered.

I blinked. Had I imagined it? I scrubbed a hand across my eyes and then gripped the wires of my cage, straining to see better.

Pip's wing stretched. Its ember-bright eyes blinked open. It shook its head and then scrambled onto its claw-paws and looked around, its tail twitching.

"Pip?" I breathed.

The knife hilt stuck in its chest quivered and then clattered to the floor.

At the sound, Crowe turned. He looked at me, then down at Pip, on the floor. His eyes narrowed, and he flinched back. "The dragon is alive," he spat out.

Oh, how could I have been so stupid? Of *course* Pip was alive! It wasn't made of flesh and blood and bone like a person or an animal. It was made of magic! A knife couldn't kill it.

Sootle, still wearing his gloves, lunged after Pip, and the little dragon leaped backward, snarling.

"Catch it!" Crowe ordered. Sootle lunged again. The other swift picked up the small tourmalifine cage.

"Get out of here, Pip!" I shouted, jumping to my feet in my cage. Then I shouted it again in the dragon language.

With both swifts grabbing after it, Pip scrambled under the table and then crawled straight up the wall and crouched at the edge of the ceiling, snarling and lashing its tail. Sootle charged after it.

"*Go!*" I shouted again, then in the dragon language, "*Valaré!*"

Pip leaped, opening its wings, and like a flaming

spear it shot across the room and blasted through one of the windows. Out into the night the dragon flew, trailing sparks and shattered glass.

After cursing at the swifts for letting Pip escape, Crowe and Nimble went out, muttering to each other, making new plans. They left Sootle on guard by the door. He had a werelight lantern turned low and the smaller tourmalifine cage on the floor next to his chair. Waiting to catch Pip in case the little dragon came back, I guessed.

I'd been stupid to think Crowe would keep a promise, but I wouldn't be stupid again. I'd fight him with everything I had.

From inside the cage there wasn't much I could do except try to escape and keep an eye on what was going on outside. This I could do with the seeing-and-hearing spell. It might work, even from inside the cage, even without me touching Pip. I'd cast the spell before the magics had settled, so it had effected with such power that all I had to do was say Pip's true name, and the spell should effect again.

I crouched in my cage, feeling the cold from the wires seeping up through my bare feet, and a chilly wind blowing in from the window Pip had smashed. I closed my eyes, concentrating.

"*Tallennar*," I whispered.

I blinked, but nothing had changed; I pricked my ears, but I still heard as a boy, not a dragon.

Try again. I stood up, facing the broken window, pressing my face up against the wire mesh of the cage. "*Tallennar!*" I shouted. My voice echoed in the attic room.

By the door, Sootle lifted his head, but he didn't get up. "Be quiet, charboy," he said.

I closed my eyes and felt the spell click into place.

When I cracked them open again, my Pip-eyes saw a dark rooftop and chimneys edged with a line of flickering flame and, far below, a court-yard and . . . something dark and ruffled. Was that water?

Wait. I knew where we were. Nimble's house

on one of the magister's islands in the river. I could throw a stone from here and hit Heartsease, just about. Pip was outside, perched on the edge of a chimney. "Pip!" I called softly.

My Pip-ears heard my own voice leaking out from the smashed-open attic window. They also heard Sootle get up from his creaky chair and take a few steps toward my cage. "What're you up to?" the swift asked.

Keeping my eyes closed, I crouched in a corner of the cage. "Nothing," I answered him.

"Hmph," he snorted, and went back to his chair and sat down.

"Go to Nevery, Pip," I whispered. "Nevery Flinglas at Heartsease." Sure as sure, Nevery was furious with me for stealing his locus stone, but if he saw Pip he'd know I was in trouble.

Pip crawled along the edge of the roof, then launched itself into the sky. My vision spiraled, and flame-edged chimneys and the roof flashed by, then, below, the river, dark and flowing, and then Heartsease loomed up. Pip shot past the big tree in the courtyard. Lights shone from the kitchen windows and upstairs, from Nevery's study and workroom. Pip swooped over the courtyard cobblestones and up the outside wall of Heartsease and landed, clinging to the bricks. The window glowed just above it. Pip crawled up the wall and peered in, pressing its snout against the window glass.

Inside, a fire burned in the hearth. Nevery's hat, cloak, and cane had been tossed in a heap on his chair. Nevery himself, dark and tall in his black suit, stood before the hearth. Benet waited by the door, his burly arms folded across his chest.

"—if you say so, sir," Benet was saying. To Pip's keen ears, his voice sounded loud, even from outside the closed window.

"I do say so," Nevery snapped. "And bring up some tea. I'll have the note ready in a moment."

Benet went out. Nevery paced before the fire, frowning and pulling at the end of his beard. "Curse it, Connwaer," he muttered. "What are you up to?"

He went to the table, cleared off his chair, pushing everything onto the floor, and sat down to dash out a note.

Benet came in with a pot of tea, cups, honey, and a plate of biscuits on a tray, which he set on the table.

"Ah, good," Nevery said. He handed Benet the note. "To Brumbee, as I said. Bring him and his apprentice straight here, no arguments."

"Yes, sir," Benet said. He headed for the door. Then he paused.

"What is it?" Nevery said.

"You think he's all right?" Benet asked.

"I think he's gotten himself into trouble, as usual," Nevery growled.

"Must've had a reason—" Benet started.

"Yes, I know, Benet," Nevery said. "To you he can do no wrong. But he's stolen my locus magicalicus. A serious problem, I hope you agree."

Benet nodded. "Yes, sir." He didn't move from the doorway. "D'you miss him, sir?"

Nevery got up from the table, still looking cross.

"Yes, of course I do." Then my Pip-ears heard him mutter something into his beard that sounded like *stupid question.*

"He might not know it," Benet said.

"What?" Nevery asked.

"Did you ever tell him?"

Nevery stared at Benet, who stood stubbornly in the doorway with his burly arms folded. After a moment, Nevery spoke. "If we're going to get the boy back"—he stopped to clear his throat—"back home, we don't have any time to waste. Go and deliver the message to the duchess."

With a glower, Benet turned and stalked out of the room. "Idiots, the both of you," my Pip-ears heard him say as he hurried down the stairs.

CHAPTER 23

My Pip-ears heard Benet slam the door to Heartsease and hurry across the cobbled courtyard.

Nevery's tea and biscuits got cold while he paced. He hadn't gotten the message from the mudlark

Den, that was clear as clear. He didn't know what I was up to, or that I needed his help, and he had no way to find me.

I'm sorry, Nevery, I wanted to say. For stealing his locus magicalicus. I knew how empty he was feeling without his locus stone and his connection to the magics. Knowing he was angry with me made me feel even more shivery cold.

After a while Nevery fetched his grimoire down from a shelf and put it on his worktable; then he brought out a scrying globe and polished it with a scrap of wormsilk cloth while he read something from the book.

What was he doing? It *looked* like he was getting things ready for the anstriker spell. But he didn't have a locus stone, so he couldn't do any magic. Even if he had his stone the spell wouldn't work, not with me shut into the tourmalifine cage.

Carefully Nevery set down the globe and found a shallow bowl. From a shelf he took a glass vial of mirror-bright slowsilver and poured it into the bowl.

He checked the grimoire again and then went to the door to listen.

They weren't coming yet. Pip's ears didn't hear anything.

"Curse it, Brumbee," Nevery muttered. "Hurry up." He paced across the floor and then back again.

After some more pacing, Pip's ears heard three people hurrying across the courtyard. Nevery heard them when the door to Heartsease opened.

He met them at the top of the stairs. Magister Brumbee, puffing and red-faced, and looking desperately worried. With him and Benet was his apprentice, Keeston, who was wearing his wizard's robe over a nightgown. Keeston's blond hair stuck up on one side of his head and was flat on the other, and he still had sleep lines from his pillow on his face.

Brumbee caught his breath. "My goodness, Nevery!" he said. "It's the middle of the night!"

"It's important," Nevery said. "My locus stone has been stolen."

Brumbee gasped. "Oh, no. But surely you took precautions."

"I thought I did," Nevery growled. I knew what he was thinking—he hadn't been expecting me to pick his pocket again. He went to the table and picked up the other two notes he'd written and brought them to Benet, by the door. "Take these now, Benet," he said.

"Yes, sir," Benet said, and left again.

Nevery pointed to Brumbee's apprentice. "You, Keeston. You've got your locus magicalicus?"

Keeston blinked and stood up straighter. "Yes, sir, I do."

Yes, he did. Because Pip had stolen it back from the chimney swifts. Now I realized the swifts must have taken Keeston's stone first as a kind of test, to see if their tourmalifine tongs and cages would work. Thanks to Pip, Keeston was able to draw out his locus stone, which he wore on a gold chain around his neck. To Pip, the stone blazed, and the flames around Keeston burned a little brighter than those around Nevery or Brumbee.

"Good." Nevery pointed to his grimoire. "Come here and take a look at this." Keeston stepped to the table.

"This is all so simply awful," Brumbee said, wringing his hands. "We still don't know who is stealing the locus magicalicii *or* what they want with them. All the magisters' stones, Nevery! Every single one!"

Nevery turned and studied Brumbee. "Not *all*, Brumbee," he said. "Conn is a magister, and his stone has not been stolen."

"Of course!" Brumbee said. "Conn. But don't you think that's, well, suspicious?"

"No, I do not," Nevery said. He pointed at the table. "There's tea and biscuits," he said, and went back to the grimoire.

"Oh," Brumbee said. He went to the other table, poured himself a cup of tea, and sank into a chair. He sipped at the tea and made a face. "It's cold!"

At the worktable, Nevery and Keeston ignored

him. "Do you see?" Nevery was saying.

Keeston gripped his locus stone. "Y-yes, sir. The anstriker spell. You're sure the magics are settled enough, sir?"

"They are, yes," Nevery said. "Can you do it?"

Keeston gulped. "I've, um, never done a spell this difficult before. Who are we escrying for?"

Nevery glanced aside at Brumbee and lowered his voice. "For Conn."

"All right." Keeston studied Nevery's grimoire for a few minutes. Nevery paced impatiently while Brumbee took nervous bites of a biscuit.

"Ready?" Nevery asked Keeston, coming to a turn in his pacing.

Keeston looked up from the grimoire. "I think so, sir. The spell is far too difficult to memorize, but I think I can read it from the page."

Inside my cage, I snorted. The anstriker wasn't *that* difficult.

"Good lad," Nevery said, and set the scrying globe in the bowl of slowsilver. Brumbee heaved himself out of the chair and crossed to the work-table to watch.

Keeston held his locus stone in one hand and rested the fingers of his other hand on the scrying globe. He started the spell, speaking slowly, reading from the grimoire. At the end he added my true name—Connwaer.

As the spell effected, the spell-spark searched, slowing when it passed over Nimble's house, where I was trapped in my cage, but the scrying globe stayed dark.

"Conn's not in Wellmet?" Keeston asked.

Nevery frowned. "He must be here," he muttered. He took two quick steps away from the table, then turned and came back. "He's hiding from the spell, curse him."

I'm not hiding from you, I wanted to shout. *I want you to find me!*

"Do the spell again, Keeston," Nevery said. "But this time escry for Conn's dragon."

Now *that* was a good idea.

"Does the dragon have a true name?" Keeston asked.

"Yes," Nevery said. "Tallennar."

"*Tallennar*," Keeston whispered.

To Pip's ears its true name sounded sharp and clear.

Keeston did the anstriker spell again and added "*Tallennar*" at the end. This time the spell-spark swirled over the city and then circled the tiny Heartsease island, landing right on top of the tiny house and flaring up brightly before flickering out.

"How strange!" Brumbee said. "The spell ended right here."

Nevery straightened, blinking the brights out of his eyes. "Because the dragon is here." He looked around the room. "Somewhere in Heartsease." He saw the window. "Or outside." He swept-stepped across the room. My Pip-eyes saw him, looming larger, and then Pip ducked its head as Nevery flung the window open.

"Ah, there you are," Nevery said, looking down

at Pip, who clung to the bricks outside. To Pip's dragon vision, Nevery looked like a shadow surrounded by the embers of flames that had gone out—because of his missing locus stone. Nevery spoke over his shoulder to Brumbee and Keeston. "Thank you for your help. You may go now."

"But Nevery!" Brumbee sputtered. "We—"

"Call a magisters meeting for midmorning," Nevery said. He pointed toward the door.

Still sputtering, Brumbee went out, followed by Keeston.

At the window, Nevery stepped aside. "Well, little Pip. Come in."

My view of the room changed as Pip crawled up and perched on the windowsill.

Nevery examined Pip. "Hmmm," he said. "You don't look very well." He reached out a hand and Pip flinched away. "All right," Nevery said. He took a step back. "Conn is in trouble, isn't he," he said quietly.

Yes, Nevery, I wanted to say. *I need your help.* I

had never asked for help before—I'd always done everything on my own—but this was too big for me.

Pip edged closer to him along the windowsill.

Nevery looked out into the night, which was just lightening to gray morning. "Curse it, boy, where are you?" He glanced down at Pip. "Perhaps you can lead me to him, Pip. We'll try—"

Bang, bang, bang!

I blinked, and the seeing-and-hearing spell faltered, and I was Conn again, huddled in the corner of the cage with my head down on my knees and the cold from the tourmalifine wires seeping into my bones, feeling sick-shivery with worry.

"What's the matter with him?" a sharp voice said. Sootle. He banged on the cage again.

I lifted my head. "What d'you want?" I asked. My voice sounded rusty.

"Breakfast," Sootle said. "Stay down there and I'll put it in."

Right. I watched as he used the keystone to open the cage, slid in a tray with breakfast on it, and closed the door again. Another swift, the woman Floss, was at the window, the one Pip had broken during the night. She held up a plank of wood and laid it across the frame and tapped in a nail to hold it in place.

On the tray was a bowl of porridge with two eggs on it this time, and an apple, and a cup of tea with curls of steam rising off it. I stared at it, stiff and cold and still getting used to seeing as Conn and not as Pip.

Nevery was being smart, trying to get Pip to lead him to me. That might work, if Nevery could get Keeston's help and figure out the right spellwords to use. He might come soon. If he did he'd better get some help from the Dawn Palace guards, maybe Kerrn and Rowan with their swords.

"You all right?" Sootle asked.

I nodded.

"Eat it, then," he said. With his foot he tapped the side of the cage.

I looked up at him. He hadn't seemed so bad

when he'd been the leader of the chimney swifts and I'd been his charboy. I'd even sort of liked him. But all along he'd been working for Crowe—and he was willing to kill for Crowe, too.

"Lied to us about your name, did you?" he said, narrowing his eyes as he stared down at me. "Not Pip at all, but Conn. Not a charboy at all, but a spying little wizard." His long nose twitched. "As young a scrap as you are, you don't look like a wizard."

Sure as sure, he thought a wizard should look like the oil paintings back in the ducal magister's rooms. I shrugged.

He frowned. "Eat your breakfast or I'll take it away."

All right. I uncurled myself from the corner and reached for the cup of tea.

Nevery would come. He'd come soon.

From the Duchess to the Underlord

Dear Embre.

It's been days since we've heard from Conn. Don't you care what happens to him? Are we supposed to sit around and wait while he gets himself into worse and worse trouble? All of these things happening at once—the locus stones missing, the troubled magics, the gangs in the city—it can't be a coincidence, and somehow Conn is the key to it all. I feel like something is about to happen, as if there is a hammer poised above the city, and we are sitting here waiting for the blow.

I just wish I knew who was holding the hammer so we could do something about it. If I have to

attend yet another meeting that produces no action I may scream.

Sincerely,
Rowan
Duchess
Dawn Palace, Sunrise

Dearest of Rowans,

We are not just *sitting around waiting*, as you say. Well, I am by necessity sitting, but I am not doing nothing. My men are on high alert, though they report nothing of Conn. The gang that has been causing trouble both here and in the Sunrise must have a base of operations. I can assure you that it is not in the Twilight. Has the palace guard scoured the Sunrise for such activity?

I expect you've heard by now from Nevery that we are to meet with him later at the Dawn Palace. Yes, O best beloved, another meeting, but I trust that once we have discussed these troubles we will think of something that needs doing. Perhaps it will involve swords and fighting, which I expect would fulfill your rather Conn-like need to act.

Yours forever,

Embre

·ꙮꚙꙷꙶꚝꙶꚛ ꙶꚙꙷꙶꚛꙶ ꚛ꙰ꙶ꙰:

CHAPTER 24

Nevery didn't come. Neither did Captain Kerrn and a troop of Dawn Palace guards, or Rowan wielding her sword, or Embre and a pack of his men.

Neither did Crowe.

I sat in my corner and shivered, watching the swift Floss finish boarding up the window. When she was done, she pulled up a chair in front of my cage. Crowe must've given her orders to keep an eye on me. I heard muffled voices and people moving around downstairs. Something was happening.

I tried to stay awake, to see if the noise would give me a clue about what was going on, but after a while I fell asleep.

When I woke up, it was late afternoon and the chimney swift was gone and the house was quiet. I pushed my face up against the cage again and said Pip's true name: *"Tallennar."*

The seeing-and-hearing spell showed me that Pip was perched in the corner of a big room. Seeing the room like that, from high up and bright with the Pip-eyes flames, made me dizzy and I closed my own eyes for a moment, then cracked them open again.

Desk cluttered with papers, tall windows, a dusty tree in a pot, comfortable chairs with lace doilies on them. Oh, I'd been there before. It was Rowan's office in the Dawn Palace. Rowan herself, wearing her duchess uniform, a green velvet dress, with her red hair hanging in an fraying braid down her back, sat behind her desk. Nevery sat in one of the comfortable chairs, and Captain Kerrn leaned against a wall with her hand on the pommel of her sword. Next to the desk sat Embre in his wheeled chair. He was pale and had dark circles under his eyes, as if he hadn't slept.

"He did *what*?" Rowan was saying.

"You heard what he said, Ro," Embre said sharply.

Rowan shot him a cross look.

"It should not be unexpected," Kerrn said. "He is a thief."

So Nevery had told them about me stealing his locus stone.

"Thief or not," Embre said, "he must've had a reason."

Yes, I'd had a reason. Not a good one, as it'd turned out.

"He must have," Rowan agreed. She took a breath and folded her hands on her desk. Calming herself so she could be duchess-like. "Magister Nevery, did Conn say anything when he picked your pocket?"

Nevery opened his mouth to answer, but a knock at the door interrupted him.

Miss Dimity poked her head into the room. "Duchess Rowan, I'm *so* terribly sorry to—"

"—to interrupt," Rowan said impatiently. "Yes, I know. What is it?"

Miss Dimity's mouth pinched with distaste. "There is a . . . *ahem* . . . a messenger here, and he *insists* on seeing Magister Nevery."

Rowan raised her eyebrows and Nevery nodded. "Show him in," he said.

Miss Dimity ushered the mudlark Den into the room, then stood behind him with her bony hand on Den's shoulder.

When I'd met him on the mudflats, Den had seemed big, like a minion-in-training, but in Rowan's office he looked grubby and hungry. He lowered his one eyebrow and glared around the room. His voice surly, he said, "I've got a message for a wizard named Never."

Nevery nodded. "I am Nevery."

Den shrugged Miss Dimity's hand off his shoulder. "Nevery, right," he said. "My message is from this piece of work gutterboy-wizard. Conn. D'you know him?"

Nevery leaned forward in his chair. "I do."

Den cast a quick look around the room, at Rowan and Embre, catching sight of Pip up in the corner of the ceiling. "Conn said to go to Heartsease, right? But you weren't there, were you? So I came here." He shrugged. "Couldn't get to you sooner. Had to get my lot settled first, and then *she*"—he nodded at Miss Dimity—"didn't want to let me in here."

Nevery looked like a kettle about to boil over. "What," he said, biting off the words, "is Conn's message?"

Den scowled at Nevery. "I'm getting to it." He rubbed his nose. "Conn says Crowe's in the city."

Nevery's eyes widened, then he nodded. "What else?"

Den shrugged. "He said to tell you it's Crowe that's been stealing the locus stones. And he said if you didn't hear from him that Crowe'd probably got him."

Rowan gasped, and Nevery went pale. Embre couldn't go any paler than he already was.

Don't worry, I wanted to tell them. *I'm all right.*

"He said Crowe would take him to a house in the Sunrise," Den went on. He pointed at Nevery. "And he said you should be careful."

"Curse the boy," Nevery muttered.

"*And*," Den went on, "he said to use the 'striker spell to find him."

"Would that work?" Rowan asked.

"I tried it last night," Nevery said, shaking his head. "It didn't work. Clearly Crowe has figured out some way to hide from the spell, and to hide Conn from us."

Ro leaped up from behind her desk and started to pace. "We must find Conn at once. We'll start by trying to find that house in the Sunrise where they're keeping him. Captain Kerrn?"

Kerrn stood alert and ready, her hand still on the pommel of her sword. "We will find him, Duchess."

Suddenly Rowan stopped pacing, and her face went very pale. "Oh. Oh, no," she whispered to herself. "We're not thinking this through. *Crowe has returned.*" Rowan gnawed at a thumbnail. "All of the magisters' locus stones have been stolen and Conn has been kidnapped, so we have no wizards to help us." She glanced at Embre. "It's quite clear, isn't it? Crowe is making a move to take over the city."

Embre was gripping the arms of his chair, his thin hands like claws. "We have to stop him." His face was white and fierce.

Rowan gave a brisk nod. "Yes, we do." She clenched her right hand, and I knew she was thinking about gripping her sword. Then she turned a bleak look on Embre. When she spoke, her voice shook. "We can't send your men or the palace guards to search for Conn."

"I know," Embre said. "I care about him, too. But you're the duchess. And I'm the Underlord. We have to protect the city first."

In my cage, Embre's words made me shiver as I realized something. I was the same as them. We were friends, me and Rowan and Embre, but the same way they had to put the city first, I had to put the magics first. It meant we could never be careful or safe; it meant we would always do what had to be done. If only I could talk to Rowan and Embre now, at this moment, I knew they would understand, and maybe Nevery would, too.

But I couldn't. Instead I squeezed my eyes tightly closed and watched what was happening in Rowan's office.

She and Embre both looked at Nevery, who'd gone to stand at the window. "I'm sorry," Rowan said, her voice shaking. "We can see that you're worried about him."

To Pip's eyes, Nevery burned less brightly, and his face looked lined and tired. He nodded, then said, "Leave finding Conn to me." He pointed at Pip. "And to—"

Poke, poke, poke.

"Is he dead?" a sharp voice asked.

Poke.

"Dunno," another voice answered.

I opened my eyes. A narrow finger reached through the wire mesh and poked my arm again.

"I'm not dead," I said in a creaky voice. I lifted my head. My cheek was cold where it'd been pressed against the tourmalifine floor of the cage. Rubbing it, I sat up.

Outside the cage crouched Sootle. Seeing me awake, he got to his feet. "Brought your dinner and a blanket," he said. "Don't give me any trouble."

I climbed stiffly to my feet. Trouble? Me?

Sootle reached into his pocket and pulled out the keystone and used it to open the cage door. Then he put the stone back into his pocket.

As he turned to fetch the dinner tray off the table, I shoved the door wider open and flung myself out of the cage. I got two steps into the room, and Sootle came after me, dropping the tray with a crash. He grabbed me. I kicked and struggled as he wrestled me back into the cage and slammed the door behind me. I crouched on the cage floor, panting. He glared down at me, then pointed at the broken dinner dishes. "No dinner for you, then, charboy." He kicked at the cage. "No blanket, neither."

"Leave him," said the swift by the door. "It's almost time."

Time for what? From downstairs came more bumps and thumps and I heard Nimble's whiny voice shout something. As Rowan had said, Crowe was planning to take over the city, and he was making his move tonight.

"Right," said Sootle, and after kicking my cage again, he left the room, followed by the other swift.

I waited until their footsteps clattered away down the stairs.

Stupid chimney swifts. They knew I was a wizard, but they'd already forgotten about my quick hands. When he'd been wrestling me back into the cage, I'd picked the keystone from Sootle's pocket.

CHAPTER 25

The keystone fit through the wire mesh, so I pushed it through with my fingers and pressed it against the corner of the cage where the door opened. Nothing happened.

"Stupid stone," I whispered.

I pulled the stone back through the wires and clenched it in my fist. Crowe was out in the city making his move, whatever it was. I needed to get *out*.

"Tallennar!" I shouted for the hundredth time. I'd tried the seeing-hearing spell and saw only darkness. Was the dragon sleeping? Wake up, Pip!

I turned to the cage to try the stone again. Steadying my fingers, I slid the keystone through the mesh. A noise from out in the hallway made my head jerk up. The stone slipped from my fingers and dropped to the floor. It bounced once and rolled away.

"Oh, curse it!" I kicked the side of the cage. Then I crouched and poked my fingers through the mesh, reaching for the stone. Too far.

The door to the attic opened. Nimble came in. I jumped to my feet and put my hands behind my back. Had he seen me trying to get the keystone?

Nimble crossed the room to stand before my cage; he was carrying a burlap sack with something in it.

I snuck a quick-look down. The keystone was just a finger length away from his foot. If he glanced at the floor, he would see it.

"Caught like a rat in a trap, aren't you, gutter-boy?" Nimble said, giving me his smirk-smile.

Oh, so he'd come to gloat. I glared at him.

"Crowe and I have arranged it so that everything that happens to the city tonight will seem like your doing. All the work of one gutterboy turned wizard who we never should have trusted because he was plotting to take over the city for himself. In the chaos after the deaths of the girl duchess and that crippled boy Underlord, Crowe and I will step in and save the city by destroying the rogue wizard Connwaer. Clever, is it not?" Nimble said. "We—"

"How d'you figure they'll think it was me?" I interrupted.

Nimble's smirk widened. "I thought of it myself. It is well known that you are interested in pyrotechnics, and that you are the only wizard in the city who can touch a locus magicalicus and survive. Thus I have created pyrotechnic devices that are set off with locus magicalicus stones." He raised the bag he was carrying and shook it. I heard the rattling sound of stones on metal—he had the stolen locus stones in a little tourmalifine cage. Sure as sure he had tourmalifine tongs in there, too, so he could handle the stones without actually touching them. "Crowe's men put the devices in place yesterday," Nimble went on. "Tonight he and I will set the locus stone fuses. The devices will destroy the Dawn Palace and Dusk House and various other strategic sites when they explode."

Wait. Explosions? *Pyrotechnics?*

My stomach lurched. "You can't do that," I said.

"Oh, and who is going to stop us?" Nimble said, scoffing at me in my cage.

I gripped the wires, their cold burning into my fingers. "No, I mean you really can't. I just settled the magics. Pyrotechnic explosions will set them off again." The magics were so huge and so different from us that they didn't even notice most of what we people did, unless a wizard got their attention with a locus stone and said a spell in the magic language.

But, maybe because they'd once been fire-breathing dragons, the magics noticed pyrotechnics. With huge explosions going off all around, the magics might be unsettled enough to clash and roil again the way they had when Arhionvar had first come to Wellmet, when fire and rocks had rained down on the city, and winds had ravaged along every street. Crowe and Nimble were taking a huge risk with their pyrotechnic devices.

"Oh, you and your nonsense about magical beings," Nimble scoffed. "The magic is simply a resource to be used." Turning to leave, his foot nudged the keystone, pushing it closer to the cage. He stalked off.

"Nimble, you can't use pyrotechnics!" I shouted after him. My heart pounded. "You could destroy the city!"

At the doorway, Nimble paused. "Truly, I am glad we did not hang you when we had the chance. You've been so much more useful to us alive. But not for long." His smirk-smile turned even nastier.

"Soon you will be more useful to us dead." Then he went out of the attic and I heard his footsteps as he trotted down the stairs.

Off he went, to set his pyrotechnic devices. This was way worse than I'd thought. I *had* to get out.

Quickly I crouched down and poked my fingers through the wires, reaching for the keystone. Nimble had kicked it closer, but not close enough. "Drats, drats, drats!" I stood up. "Pip!" I shouted again.

This time, Pip answered. I heard a scrabbling at one of the low windows, and then one of the glass panes shattered and Pip poked its snout in and looked around, checking for chimney swifts, I guessed. Then it squeezed in the window and crawled down the wall and across the floor toward me.

"Pip!" I gasped. "I need you to get me out of here." The dragon could pick up the keystone and use it to open the cage.

Pip stopped next to the stone and fixed me with

one of its red glare-stares.

"The stone," I said, crouching down and poking my fingers through the wires, pointing at the stone. "See the keystone right there?"

Pip blinked.

I said it again in the dragon language so it could understand better. *Tallennar take keystone, open cage?* I asked it. To anyone listening, it would've sounded like I'd just said a magical spell.

Pip leaned over and picked up the keystone in its mouth.

"Oh, please don't swallow it," I whispered.

Holding the stone, Pip edged closer to the cage. It put a claw-paw on the tourmalifine wires. Sparks flared up, snap-crackling, and Pip flinched away, dropping the stone.

Oh, no. I'd forgotten. Pip's scales were made of slowsilver, so when the dragon touched the tourmalifine wires, it got hurt.

I gulped down a knot of desperation. "You don't have to do it, Pip."

Ignoring me, Pip picked up the stone again and, with sparks dash-flashing all around it, scrambled up the side of the cage and held the keystone against the corner. As the cage cracked open, Pip dropped the stone and fell to the floor in a shower of sparks, panting.

I shoved open the cage door and went to crouch next to Pip. "You all right?" I asked.

As an answer, Pip spat out a glimmering glob of light that charred the wooden floorboards it touched, then climbed up my arm to cling to my shoulder. I turned my head and lay my face against Pip's warm scales. "Thanks for coming back," I whispered.

Deep in its chest, the little dragon purred.

All right, then.

I got to my feet. Now that I was out of the tourmalifine cage, I could feel all around me the strong, stony Arhionvar magic and the softer, old Wellmet magic. They were still settled from the talking-to I'd given them, Arhionvar over the Sunrise, the old magic over the Twilight, meeting here on the wizards' islands in the middle of the river. But the magics felt as if the slightest push would set them roiling and swirling against each other. Pyrotechnic devices exploding all over the city—that wouldn't be a slight push, it'd be disaster. I raced down the stairs, looking for Nimble.

The house was empty.

CHAPTER 26

Outside Nimble's house, the day was ending. Pip dropped to the cobblestones in the court-yard and glared at the flames and shadows cast by the setting sun.

"There he is," I heard Nevery's gravelly voice say, and then he swept-stepped around a corner of the house, Benet behind him gripping a truncheon.

Nevery looked me up and down. "You're all right, my lad?"

I took a shivery breath. The

last time I'd seen him . . .

"Nevery, I'm very sorry about stealing your locus stone," I said.

"Hmm, yes," he said. "I expect you are. Crowe tricked you into it, did he?"

I nodded. He had, curse him.

"It's all right, my lad," Nevery said, and rested a hand on my shoulder.

I would make it all right. When I got his locus stone back.

"Anybody after you?" Benet put in, pointing at the house.

I shook my head. "They've all gone."

"Good," Nevery said. "Well done, little Pip." Nevery nodded at Pip, who was crouched at my feet. "Your dragon led us to you, Connwaer. We would have been here sooner, but—"

"Never mind that, Nevery," I interrupted. Quickly I told him what I knew, that Nimble had hidden his sneaky locus-stone pyrotechnic devices in the Dawn Palace and Dusk House, and in other places, too. Nevery raised his eyebrows when he heard that Nimble—another magister—was involved in Crowe's plot, but he nodded at me to continue. "He's using the locus stones as fuses," I explained, and told him that Nimble had left not long ago to set the fuses. Crowe also had a houseful of minions and his chimney swifts to make trouble. He planned to blow up Rowan in the Dawn Palace and Embre in Dusk House and take over the city. "We have to hurry," I finished. Night was coming, and that's when Crowe would make his move.

While I explained, Benet led us to the dock where he'd tied the boat he and Nevery had rowed across in, from Heartsease.

"Wait," I said, thinking of something that could save us time. "I have to look for something."

"Boy—" Nevery began.

"I'll come right back," I promised, and with Pip flying behind, I raced across the cobbles to Nimble's house, then up the stairs to the floor just below the attic. When I'd been in the cage, I'd heard Nimble shouting at people, Crowe's minions and swifts probably, and it'd sounded like it'd come from there. "*Lothfalas*," I said, for some light, and tried doorknobs. Four rooms were empty except for tumbled blankets and pillows and smelly socks and some other junk. Clear as clear, more than just a few chimney swifts had been sleeping in these rooms. Crowe must have snuck more minions into the city, too, and they'd been hiding out here.

The fifth room was locked. This had to be it, Nimble's workroom. "Pip," I called, and the dragon came closer, bringing the hazy glow of the lothfalas light with it. I got out my lockpick wires and—*quick hands*—picked the lock.

What I was hoping to find was a map of Wellmet, maybe with the locations of the hidden pyrotechnic-locus-stone devices conveniently marked on it.

Nimble's workroom had a long table in it, and a desk piled with papers, and books piled on the floor in teetering stacks, and leaky boxes and bulging bags and vials with labels on them that said things like *saltpeter* and *tourmalifine powder* and *sulfur*.

This was where Nimble had been doing his experiments, where he'd made the tourmalifine cages, and where he'd been working out how to make locus-stone pyrotechnic devices.

Moving as fast as I could without bumping something, I went to the desk and looked through the papers. No map. Then to a sloppy pile of papers on the floor next to the desk. No map there, either.

Drats, I didn't have time for this!

I tiptoed to the worktable and shuffled through the papers strewn across it. Nothing.

I was on my knees digging through a box of junk next to the desk when I heard a heavy *step, step, step* in the hallway, and Benet pushed his way in.

"Come on, you," he growled.

I carefully set a jumble of tourmalifine wires on the floor. "Just stay over there by the door, Benet," I said. "The room's full of pyrotechnic materials."

Benet had a very good reason for not liking pyrotechnics; he'd been hurt by them the first time I'd accidentally blown up Heartsease. He went still, and when he spoke, his lips hardly moved. "We can't leave Master Nevery waiting. He's been worried."

"I know," I said. I'd seen him through Pip's eyes, though Benet didn't know that. And I thought Nevery was more annoyed with me than worried.

"Ask him to tell you," Benet said.

"Tell me what?" I asked.

"He knows," Benet said, and I knew him well enough to know that he wasn't going to say any more. "You coming?"

I nodded and pulled a rag-wrapped bundle out of the box. Tourmalifine tongs. They weren't as good as a map, but they'd be useful for defusing Nimble's pyrotechnic devices, if the devices worked the way I guessed they did. Keeping the tongs close to me so I didn't knock over a vial of slowsilver and blow us both up, I got to my feet and edged out of the room. Benet and I hurried down the dark stairs and, followed by Pip, out to the boat where Nevery was not very patiently waiting.

The question was where to go first. The sun was going down behind the steep streets of the Twilight, and flames of light streaked the sky. Darkness was spreading from the east, over the Sunrise part of the city.

Nimble was out there setting the fuses in his pyrotechnic devices. I had to stop him, and I had to keep the devices he'd already set from exploding. But where had he started?

"Come along, boy," Nevery growled from the boat.

I shook my head, still standing on the dock, gripping the tongs. Embre was at Dusk House; Rowan was at the Dawn Palace. They were both in danger; I had to get them both to safety. But where first?

I knew what I had to do. Ask for help.

That decided, I jumped into the boat; Pip flapped in after me. "We have to go to the mudflats on the Twilight side. And we have to hurry."

A nod from Nevery, and Benet pushed the boat into the river's current, gripped the oars, and started rowing.

"What's your plan, boy?" Nevery asked, grabbing the side of the boat as a wave sloshed against it.

"Nevery, I can stop some of Nimble's devices from blowing up by taking out the locus stone fuses," I explained. Because unlike anybody else in the city, I could touch a locus stone and not be killed. I held out the tongs and Nevery took them.

He looked them over, frowning. "What are they made of?" he asked. Even in the dim light, the metal the tongs were made from had a greeny sheen.

As the dark bulk of Nimble's house on its island receded behind us, I told Nevery how Nimble had used tourmalifine wires to hide Crowe—and me—from the anstriker spell, and how he'd made these tongs so he could pick up the locus stones. "Because tourmalifine repels magic. D'you see, Nevery?"

"Yes, I see," he answered. "Very clever. I can use these tongs to defuse some of the pyrotechnic devices, by taking out the locus stones, is that what you're thinking?"

I nodded. "You'll have to be very careful, Nevery."

He gave me one of his keen-gleam looks. "Really, boy."

Really. But Nevery knew how to pick locks. I'd taught him myself. He had steady hands, and he could defuse a device without getting himself blown up.

"Do you know where Nimble's hidden the devices?" Nevery asked.

I didn't know, but I could guess. There would be one device for each magister's locus stone that had been stolen by the chimney swifts. Not counting me, there were six magisters all together: Nevery, Sandera, Trammel, Brumbee, Periwinkle, and Nimble. My stone was in Pip, and Nimble wouldn't have put his own stone into one of the devices. Five stolen locus stones; that meant five explosive devices. Sure as sure there were devices hidden in the Dawn Palace and Dusk House. That left three more devices. Where had Nimble put them?

"Just get the one in Dusk House," I told Nevery. I would worry about the rest of them. Then I told him a little more about how I guessed Nimble had made the pyrotechnic devices and what Nevery

would have to do to defuse them, and how dangerous they'd be to the magics if they went off, and
by the time we got to the mudflats, the last of the
sunset flames were dying in the sky. Benet beached
the boat.

"Wait here," Nevery said to him as we climbed
out.

My bare feet sank deep into the smelly mud; I
slopped through it with Nevery beside me steadying
himself by gripping my shoulder. Pip flew ahead.
We pushed through tall reeds to the path that led
along the mudflats.

"Nevery, you won't get to Dusk House without help," I said, hurrying down the path. Crowe
had been the Underlord before, and he had to hate
Embre more than anyone; it made sense that he'd
start his attacks in the Twilight. That part of the
city would be crawling with Crowe's minions and
the chimney swifts, and Nevery didn't have a locus
stone to defend himself with.

As we came to the mudlarks' shack, Pip flew up

and perched on my shoulder. Smoke was trickling from the shack's tin stovepipe. We were in luck; they were there.

Before I could knock on the door, it opened, and Den stepped out. Jo stood behind him, her face pale.

"What d'you want now, wizard boy?" Den asked, his narrow eyes flicking quick glances over me and Pip, and then over Nevery.

"You know Crowe's come back," I answered. Then I quickly explained how Crowe was making his move to take over the city tonight. "Nevery has to get to Dusk House," I went on. "So he can save Underlord Embre and start fighting Crowe on this side of the river."

Den hesitated, as if he was deciding.

Then, from behind, Jo poked him. "It's the gutterboy-wizard asking," she whispered. "He was like us, Den."

"All right, we'll help," Den said. "We'll fight Crowe and any of his minions he's brought back with him." He gave a sudden fierce grin. "Crowe's a bad lot. He used to send men to beat the fluff out of us mudlarks when we didn't pay him off. We don't want him running the city again." He poked his head into the shack. "Come on, you kids!" he shouted to the other mudlarks hiding there.

As the kids came blinking out of the dark shack into the last of the daylight, I stepped away, ready to head for Benet so he could row me over to the Sunrise. I could almost feel the sun pulling the darkness across the sky as it sank away. I had to get to Rowan at the Dawn Palace *soon*.

Nevery stopped me with a hand on my shoulder. "From what you tell me, Connwaer, Nimble's devices are extremely dangerous."

I wouldn't tell him I'd be careful. He knew I couldn't be; not now, with the city and the magics in such terrible danger. "I'll have Pip with me," I said. On my shoulder, Pip gave a low growl. "I have to hurry, Nevery."

He let me go. "As do I," he said. "Go."

I went.

CHAPTER 27

T he guards at the front doors of the Dawn
Palace tried to stop me as I sprinted up the
steps.

I could hardly blame them. I looked like a gutterboy—barefoot, wearing rags and my black sweater,

covered with mud and soot-smudges, panting from racing up the hill from the river. "I'm a wizard," I shouted at them. On my shoulder, Pip arched its back, snorting out sparks and smoke, lashing its tail. "Out of my way!"

They got out of my way. I shoved open the double doors and raced inside. Rowan. I had to find her.

Striding down the echoing hallway came Captain Kerrn, two palace guards behind her. She snapped out an order to the guards and they advanced on me.

"No, Kerrn!" I shouted, skidding to a stop. Oh, please listen. "Rowan's in danger."

She held up a hand, and the guards paused.

"Where is she?" I panted.

"This way," Kerrn said briskly. She led me down a hallway, pointing at a door at its end. I charged ahead of her and flung open the door.

Inside was a table with a few of the city councilors, palace guards, Miss Dimity, and Brumbee standing around it; Rowan stood at its head. On the table was a map of the city. They all looked up as I burst into the room; Miss Dimity gave a little shriek.

"Ro!" I shouted. "You have to get out of here."

Rowan took off her golden spectacles and raised her eyebrows. The others at the table were exclaiming, and the guards put their hands on their sword pommels and scowled.

"What is it, Conn?" Rowan asked, crossing the room to me.

Kerrn shoved me around to face her. "Yes, what?" Her ice-chip eyes were fierce.

"Get everybody out," I said. "Out of the Dawn Palace." They both stared. Drats; I had to explain again. I caught my breath. "Nimble's been working with Crowe. He's set an explosive device in the palace. It could go off anytime."

Rowan nodded. "Do as Conn says, Kerrn; get everybody out."

Kerrn was already issuing orders; her guards were hustling the other people out of the room. More guards came rushing in, and Kerrn sent them to search the rest of the palace.

"Hurry!" I said, pulling Rowan toward the door.

"Yes, all right," she said, and strode along beside me. She'd already started thinking it through. "Crowe is making his move tonight," she said, as we hurried down the hallway to the main doors. "He'll start with the Twilight. Is Embre all right?"

"I don't know," I answered. "There's a device at Dusk House, too. Nevery's gone to get Embre out."

Rowan's face went very pale. "Oh, no."

As we stepped outside, with a view over the river to the Twilight, a blinding burst of light exploded from one of the wizards' islands. Then another flash, white-bright against the night. Sparks blasted into the darkness. A roar of sound rolled over us.

One of the pyrotechnic devices had gone off.

Rowan gasped. People streamed past us, fleeing the Dawn Palace, some of them screaming, others babbling with fright.

Somebody bumped into me and Rowan, and then Kerrn was there.

"Captain," Rowan said, as Kerrn hustled her farther away from the building, "ready what guards we have. We must defend the city."

I stood on the steps, trying to see above people's heads. In the distance, sparks were still flying up from the island, and a glowing cloud of smoke billowed up; flames flickered. It was Nimble's house that had exploded, I realized. A cold feeling gathered in my stomach. I was supposed to be in there—if I hadn't gotten out of the cage I'd have been blown to bits.

On my shoulder, Pip leaned toward the explosion, quivering with excitement. Smoke trickled up from its tiny nostrils. Overhead, I felt the huge magic of Arhionvar shift as it reacted to the pyrotechnics. It held its place over the Sunrise. But its hold was precarious. We couldn't risk another explosion.

"Come away, Ducal Magister," Kerrn said. She stood two steps below me. A few last people and guards hurried past us, fleeing.

I shook my head. "Wait," I said. I knew where

Nimble had hidden the pyrotechnic device. He wanted me to seem guilty; he must've snuck in and put it in the ducal magister's rooms. "I have to defuse the device," I said.

Kerrn shook her head. "You cannot risk your life for a building," she said sharply.

It wasn't the Dawn Palace I was worried about. For one thing, if the device exploded it'd take a magister's locus stone with it. Nevery's stone, maybe. I couldn't let that happen. For another, I couldn't let another explosion trouble the magics. "Keep everybody away," I told her. Just in case. Then I turned and raced back into the palace.

CHAPTER 28

Nimble hadn't even bothered to hide the pyrotechnic device. It was sitting on the patterned carpet in the ducal magister's room, a plain wooden box with handles and a lid on it, small enough that I could have heaved it up and carried it in my arms.

But I didn't want to do that.

Krrrr, Pip said into my ear. *Hurry*, it meant.

I crept across the room and knelt next to the box. The oil-painted magisters on the walls frowned down at me. "*Lothfalas*," I whispered, and Pip breathed out a glowing ball of sparks that hovered overhead. Carefully—*steady hands*—I lifted the top off the box and peered inside.

It was as I'd suspected. The box was packed with blackpowder explosives. On top of the blackpowder, glowing bright green against the black, was a heap of tourmalifine crystals with a locus magicalicus sitting on it. Brumbee's round, brown locus stone; it looked like a hen's egg in a green nest. Near the heap of tourmalifine was a saucer full of slowsilver, shimmering like a liquid mirror in the dim light. That was the fuse. The idea was, the slowsilver would be attracted to the locus stone, so it would creep out of the dish toward the stone in its pile of tourmalifine. When slowsilver and tourmalifine mingled, they exploded. That smaller explosion would set off the huge blackpowder explosion.

The slowsilver had already crept partway out of the saucer; slowly it oozed toward the pile of tourmalifine crystals. Only a finger's width separated them. When the slowsilver touched the tourmalifine—*BOOM!*

Taking a deep breath, I stilled my hands and reached into the box. Pip climbed up to perch on my head to watch, clinging to my hair.

"Pip, your tail is in my eyes," I whispered. The dragon shifted so I could see, but still leaned toward the box.

Carefully, so carefully, I touched Brumbee's locus stone. It felt cool and smooth, and I could feel the magic in it, too, a prickling in the tips of my fingers. With steady hands I eased the stone from its nest of tourmalifine crystals, then held it over each flowing bit of slowsilver, slowly coaxing it back into the saucer. When every silver-bright snail was inside, I put Brumbee's locus stone down on the floor, then reached in and, careful not to spill a drop, lifted out the saucer of slowsilver and set it down outside the box.

I sat back and let out a shivery breath. There, I'd done it. The device was defused.

Pip started to hop down, going after the locus stone, but I snatched away the stone and put it in my pocket, grabbed Pip and stood, my legs shaking, then set off running through the echoing passages of the Dawn Palace and out the front doors.

The courtyard outside was deserted. I stood with Pip in my arms on the steps and looked out over the city. Night had fallen. In the dark distance where the river ran through the middle of the city, sparks and orange smoke still drifted up from the island where Nimble's house had stood. Pip squirmed in my hands, so I let it go, and it dropped to the ground and glared up at me. The dragon was a magical creature; it had wanted that locus stone for itself.

"Sorry, Pip," I said, and started down the palace steps.

Rowan, followed by Kerrn and Miss Dimity and a few more palace guards, hurried to meet me at the bottom. Rowan had gotten a sword from somewhere; she wore it belted over her green dress. "Conn!" she shouted. "Did you—"

"Yes," I answered. I'd defused the device, I meant.

"What now?" Rowan asked. Beside her, Kerrn gripped her sword.

"My dear duchess," Miss Dimity said, bulging her eyes at Rowan's sword. "I really don't think you should—"

"Quiet," Rowan said, holding up her hand. "No interruptions."

Miss Dimity looked as if she'd swallowed a frog.

I glanced toward the Twilight. No smoke, no fire. So Dusk House hadn't exploded. Yet. "Nevery's defusing the pyrotechnic device at Dusk House."

Rowan gave a brisk nod. "Captain Kerrn's guards are reporting that Crowe's minions have been pouring into the Twilight. The first explosion was a signal to them, apparently." She looked over her shoulder at the billows of smoke and sparks still coming from the island. "We have things under control in the Sunrise." She turned back to me. "I need to help Embre."

Yes, she did. I told her and Kerrn where to find Benet, who was waiting at the riverbank with the boat.

"Benet's there?" Kerrn asked, brightening.

"Yes," I answered. "He can row you over to the Twilight to join the fight."

"Good," Rowan said. "You're coming with us, Conn?"

"No. I think I know where Crowe has planted one of the other pyrotechnic bombs. I have to go defuse it." I turned to hurry away.

Rowan took my arm, stopping me, and she didn't look quite so duchessly. "Listen, Conn," she whispered quickly. "I'm sorry about making you the ducal magister, and then trying to make you stay safe inside. We all decided we knew what was best for you, even though you kept saying you didn't want it." She gave me a wry smile. "You don't talk a lot, you know, so when you do, we ought to listen."

"It's all right, Ro," I said. Because suddenly, it was.

"Friends again?" she asked.

"Friends always," I said. "And I have to go."

She nodded and opened her mouth to say something, but I answered for her. "I can't be careful, Ro—you know that. It's for the magics—and the city."

She gave me a grim nod. "Yes, Conn, I know. Now go."

I figured Crowe was trying to destroy the centers of power in Wellmet. If he wanted to strike at the wizards, he'd plant a pyrotechnic device at Magisters Hall, on one of the islands in the river.

With Pip clinging to my shoulder, I started down the wide streets of the Sunrise, heading for the Night Bridge. A few guard patrols were out, but the streets were mostly quiet and the houses were locked up tight. Everything was happening across the river.

At the bridge I slowed to see if any swifts or minions were about. The bridge had houses built on it, and the road ran through the middle of them; in the night it looked like the mouth of a tunnel leading into darkness. Keeping my ears pricked, I padded onto the bridge and, hearing nothing but my own quiet footsteps, hurried to the stairs leading to the secret tunnel that led from the bridge to the magisters' islands in the river. Down I went, trying not to let my bare feet slide off the slippery steps.

"*Lothfalas*," I said as I entered the tunnel, and greenish light flared around me and Pip. I made for the first gate, said the spell to go through, and raced along the dripping tunnel to the stairs leading up to the island.

When I reached the top of the stairs, I let the lothfalas light go out. No sense in telling Crowe and Nimble I was here in case *they* were here. The hallway I'd come out in was dark.

I searched the rest of the building, and it was

dark, too, and quiet. I peeked into offices and meeting rooms, cellars and storage rooms, and found no strange boxes full of blackpowder and locus stone fuses.

Drats. This was taking too *long*!

I rushed out the front door of Magisters Hall to the slate-stone courtyard that lay before it. To the west, the Twilight was dark as a bruise, with points of light in the houses and, higher up near Dusk House, brighter smudges—torches. No explosion yet.

I had to see how Nevery was getting on. Maybe I needed to go there next. I had time, if I made it quick. "Pip," I whispered. "Go spy on Nevery and then come back here." I said it again in the dragon language. Then I said *"Tallennar"* to start the seeing-and-hearing spell again. The spell-spark flared and I saw and heard the world as Pip did.

Pip leaped from my shoulder into the air. A whirl of sky and stars, and then I saw the dark water of the river rushing underneath as Pip flew across the river, heading for the Twilight. To our right, the rubble of Nimble's house on its island lit up the sky with a red glow; to the left loomed the dark bulk of the Night Bridge. My Pip-ears could hear, coming from the steep streets of the Twilight, shouts and screams and the sounds of running feet.

As Pip flew, I felt the Arhionvar magic overhead, pushing toward Nimble's house, where the last explosion had happened; the softer Wellmet magic felt twitchy, like a horse getting spooked. They felt like they were just about to tip over into chaos.

Hurry, Pip, I thought.

Pip shot over the dark streets up to Dusk House. The house was lit up with torches; in their flickering orange light, I caught a quick glimpse of men and women fighting in front of its doors, the flash of knives and clubs swinging, Crowe's chimney swifts and his minions charging forward, and Embre's men pushing them back, helped by mudlarks and gutterkids; I saw the mudlark Den pry up a cobblestone from the street and hurl it at Crowe's men. There was no sign of Crowe, but Embre was in the thick of it, gripping a knife and shouting an order to one of his men while his aunt Sparks tried to push his wheeled chair through the crowd, farther away from Dusk House.

Then I heard Rowan shout, "Embre!" She drew her sword.

As Embre heard Rowan and looked toward her, a chimney swift holding a knife lunged at him; with a shout, Rowan leaped between them, her sword flashing in the dim light. Kerrn followed, sword drawn, with Benet beside her, elbowing a minion in the face, then swinging his truncheon. The minions and swifts before them fell back.

Embre shot a wild glance at Pip as the dragon flew over his head and into the building. Pip darted down one corridor, then dodged into a side door and flew up to the room's ceiling and clung there. A storage room, it looked like, full of boxes and barrels.

In one corner, Nevery, who was holding the tourmalifine tongs, and the mudlark Jo were peering into a big wooden box—much bigger than the one Nimble had hidden in the Dawn Palace.

"Ah," I heard Nevery say, and he pointed at something in the box.

Go closer, Pip.

Pip crawled along the ceiling until it was right over Nevery and Jo and the explosive device. I got a good look at what was inside.

Oh, no. *Get out of there, Nevery!* I wanted to shout at him.

This fuse was much closer to exploding than the one in the Dawn Palace device. As before, a locus magicalicus—Periwinkle's gray river stone—sat on a pile of tourmalifine crystals. But this time the mirror-bright slowsilver snails had almost reached the tourmalifine. Not a fingernail's width separated them. Another second, and they would mingle and explode.

As I watched, Nevery reached in with the tongs, and—

BOOM!

I blinked and Nevery in Dusk House disappeared, and I had time to take a quick breath before a wave of wind and burning air slammed me to the slate stones of the Magisters Hall courtyard. Under me, the ground rumbled, and a huge gout of flames and smoke burst into the air, brilliant orange against the night sky. The roaring boom of an explosion rumbled over the city, followed by a hot, smoky wind.

Overhead, the Arhionvar magic shifted like giant stones getting ready to thunder downhill in an avalanche.

My heart gave a lurch. *Oh, no.* Not Dusk House, not Nevery.

The ground was still shivering as I got to my feet, searching the Twilight for the explosion. But no; this explosion had come from behind me. I whirled to look. Where the dark bulk of the Night Bridge had stood was now a raging ruin of fire, sparks, smoke. From that direction, I heard people screaming and the crackle of flames.

That was four devices accounted for: the one in Dusk House, the one I'd defused in the Dawn Palace, the one on the bridge, and the first one to go off in Nimble's house.

That meant there was just one pyrotechnic device left to find. I could feel time running out as Crowe and Nimble set its fuse. But where was it? Where?

As I turned, searching the light-spangled darkness that was the Twilight, and then the Sunrise, I saw it. Across the water, the next island after Nimble's. Lights were moving inside a building that should've been dark.

Crowe and Nimble. They were there, in Heartsease.

In my home.

CHAPTER 29

I had to stop Crowe and Nimble from blowing up Heartsease, and I couldn't wait for Pip to get back from Dusk House to do it. And I couldn't get to Heartsease through the tunnel gates, not without Pip to open the magic locks for me.

I needed a boat. Quick as sticks, I raced across the courtyard to the docks where rowboats were tied for people who weren't wizards and didn't use the secret tunnels. Grabbing the first boat I came to, I untied the rope and shoved out into the dark river water, then dropped the oars into the locks and started rowing toward the lights of Heartsease.

As I rowed, a storm gathered overhead. Slowly clouds started to turn like a giant wheel over the city, heavy green and black, pressing lower and lower. Behind me, a bolt of wind shrieked past; I turned to look and saw it rip over the water, leaving a froth of white waves in its wake. When the wind reached the Twilight shore, it smashed through a warehouse, and I heard the sound of windows shattering. Another blast of wind followed, and this time fire flared where it hit the shore.

The magics were reacting to the pyrotechnics—just as I'd warned Nimble. Time was slipping away. If another pyrotechnic device went off, controlling the magics would be like trying to stop a tornado by gripping its whirling end. The magics would sweep through the city; there'd be whirlwinds and flaming rocks falling from the sky, and the river would surge out of its banks. I wouldn't be able to stop it if it got that bad.

Turning back to the oars, I rowed as hard as I could. The river water grew choppy from the howling wind, and I could feel the magics roiling overhead. Finally the boat bumped up against the black rocks that lined the Heartsease island and I leaped out, then ran past the dark-branched tree and across the cobbled courtyard, keeping an eye out for chimney swifts or minions. The branches of the black tree thrashed in the wind. Most of Heartsease was dark, but lights gleamed from the second floor. Nevery's study.

Quick I skiffed up the stairs, then paused at the study door to catch my breath. From outside came the sound of the wind screaming around Heartsease. But no thunder, no lightning—it wasn't that kind of storm. I had to hurry before it got worse.

Crowe had to be in there, and Nimble. They probably had swifts with them. Without Pip I didn't have magic, but I was a good thief. I had quick hands, steady hands, and I could melt into shadows, and I could stop them—if I was careful.

Holding my breath, I turned the knob and eased open the study door, just a crack big enough to spy through.

Inside the room, I saw a sliver of bookshelf and wavery light coming from a single candle set on the long, wooden table that Nevery and I liked to work at in the evenings. The rest of the room was dark with shadows.

I pushed the door open a little wider. There, over by the fireplace. Crowe had his back to me. He was standing next to Nimble, who was bent over a wooden box with iron handles on it, for carrying. Its wooden lid was off. The pyrotechnic device.

And *there*—on the table behind Nimble. A glass vial full of mirror-bright slowsilver, gleaming in the dim candlelight.

So they hadn't set the fuse yet. All I needed to do was get into the room, snatch the vial, and dump it out so they couldn't use the slowsilver for their locus stone fuse.

Edging closer to the door, I scanned as much of the room as I could see. Had they come without minions or chimney swifts? I couldn't see any big, burly men lurking in the shadows. Maybe they'd sent them to fight at Dusk House. All the better for me.

I pushed the door open wider, wide enough so I could slip through. Neither Crowe nor Nimble noticed; they had their backs to me and were focused on the pyrotechnic bomb.

"Hand me the tongs," I heard Nimble say. The house shuddered as another gust of wind howled past the island. I couldn't wait any longer.

As Crowe reached into a bag he was carrying, I darted inside and faded into the shadows at the edge of the room. On cat feet, I crept toward the table and the vial of slowsilver.

"Get on with it," Crowe said. He put his hand in his pocket, and I heard the *tick-tick-tick* of his calculating device.

As I slipped closer and got ready to spring for the slowsilver, a bony hand clamped over my mouth and a snakelike arm went around my throat.

"Mfff!" I got out, and struggled, but the arms held me tightly.

Crowe and Nimble whirled to look.

"Caught a rat sneaking in," the man holding me grunted. It was Sootle.

I kicked at him, and he lifted me off my feet, his arm tightening around my neck. Black spots swirled in front of my eyes.

"I thought you said he was dead," I heard Crowe's cold voice say.

"He is!" Nimble shrieked. "He couldn't have survived the explosion at my house on the island."

"Apparently he did," Crowe said. "Put him down," he ordered Sootle. "But hold him tightly. He's slippery."

Sootle set me on my feet and took his hand away from my mouth, and I gasped for breath. He kept his other arm wrapped around my neck and grabbed my arm and wrenched it behind me so I couldn't move.

"Well, well." Crowe stepped closer. "You do like to upset my most careful calculations, don't you, Connwaer. But I don't think you're going to get away this time." He gazed at me for a few moments, and then gave me a cold smile. "In fact, I don't think you're going to like this very much at all." He glanced at Nimble. "Go down and fetch some rope from the boat. And be sure he didn't bring anybody with him."

Nimble set down the tourmalifine tongs he'd been holding and went out the door.

"Hm." Crowe scanned the room, then looked back at me. "Where is your dragon, Connwaer? Has it abandoned you?"

I didn't answer. Looking past him, I saw the vial of slowsilver, still sitting on the table. All I had to do was knock it over. . . .

I wriggled, but Sootle gripped me even more tightly.

Crowe gave a dry laugh. "You do like to struggle, don't you?"

I heard footsteps on the stairs, and Nimble appeared carrying a coil of rope. "Bit of wind out there," he reported, looking rumpled and pale.

"It's more than a bit of wind," I put in.

"Keep quiet," Sootle hissed into my ear.

"It's just a storm," Crowe said shortly. "Did he come alone?"

"Yes, he's alone," Nimble said.

"Of course he is," Crowe said, taking the rope. "If there's one thing I've learned about my nephew here, it's that he's exceptionally stupid about charging into dangerous situations all by himself."

I wanted to protest—I was getting a lot better at asking for help when I needed it—but this was something I *had* to do to protect the magics. Nobody else could do it for me.

Crowe pointed at the box. "Finish setting the fuse," he ordered Nimble. He motioned Sootle forward. "Bring him closer so he can see."

As Sootle dragged me closer, I tried kicking out at the vial of slowsilver, but missed. Sootle jerked my arm higher behind my back. "You can't do this," I gasped.

"Keep still, little charboy," Sootle hissed.

"Oh, he'll keep still in a few minutes," Crowe said gloatingly. "Very, very still."

My heart started pounding harder. What were they going to do with me?

"I need the locus stone," Nimble said, from where he was crouched by the box.

"You have to listen," I said, as dread shuddered through me. "If this device goes off, it'll destroy the whole city."

Crowe had taken the box made of tourmalifine wires from his bag. Inside it, small and dark as a soft-edged bit of night, was Nevery's locus stone. Crowe paused, and his cold eyes examined me. "What is he talking about, Nimble?"

"Don't listen to him," Nimble said in his whiny voice. "He's a nosy gutterboy who doesn't know the first thing about magic. Now, I need that stone."

Crowe nodded. Carefully he opened the tourmalifine box, and Nimble reached in with the tourmalifine tongs. He picked up the stone and brought it to the bigger wooden box.

The box was packed with blackpowder that looked blacker than ink in the dim room. Just like in the other pyrotechnic devices, there was a pile of tourmalifine, shining green crystals in the middle of the inky black. Set around the tourmalifine were three empty saucers.

Holding the tongs tightly, Nimble set Nevery's locus stone into its little nest of tourmalifine crystals. Then he put the tongs on the floor.

As he picked up the vial of slowsilver, his hands shook. He'd never make a good thief or lockpick.

"Get on with it," Crowe snapped.

Slowly Nimble poured slowsilver into each of the waiting saucers. The slowsilver swirled and sparked. "There," he said in his whiny voice. "The fuse is set."

Crowe handed him the wooden lid, and Nimble put it carefully on the box; then Crowe turned to me. "Now, Connwaer, I want you to kneel beside the box."

"No," I said, and tried squirming out of Sootle's grip, my shoulder shooting fire as he wrenched my arm back again.

"Don't be stupid," Crowe said, holding up a chiding finger. "If you struggle, you'll bump the box, and set off the explosion." He smiled. "You don't want to do that, do you?"

No, I didn't. I had no choice. With Sootle still gripping me by the shoulders, I knelt beside the box. It came up to the middle of my chest.

"Lean over the box," Crowe ordered.

I did as he said, very careful not to bump it. Sootle's hand clamped down on the back of my neck, keeping me in place. Crowe grabbed one of my hands and, using the rope Nimble had brought up from the boat, lashed my wrist to the iron handle on one side of the box. Then he did the same on the other side.

"All right," he said, and Sootle's hand let me go.

And there I was, tied to the pyrotechnic device. When it exploded, I would explode with it, and the magics would rip through the city until there was nothing left of it.

I heard Nimble gathering his things, and Sootle thump down the staircase, followed by Nimble's lighter hurrying footsteps. When they opened the door, I heard the howl of the wind and then a shrieking crash as it slammed into a building in the Twilight. Ignoring the noise, Crowe stood in the middle of the room, watching me. "This has such a satisfying rightness about it," he said, with a thin sliver of a smile.

"I could bump it right now," I said. The box, I meant. Blow myself up, and take Crowe with me.

"You could," Crowe said calmly, almost as if we were having an ordinary conversation. "But I don't think you will. Because I know you, Nephew, and I know you're always looking for a way out. Up to now, you've found it. But this time I think your luck has run out."

Drats, he was right about that. For me and the magics.

Crowe bent so he was looking straight into my eyes. "Now, Connwaer," he said. His hand went into his pocket, and I heard the *tick-tick* of the clicker device. "You don't have much time before the device explodes, and you'll want to cling to every second. You cannot do anything except stay very, very still."

With that, he left.

CHAPTER 30

I stayed very, very still. The edge of the box dug into my chest. My arms felt stretched tight, and the ropes tying me to the handles bit into my wrists. I took shallow breaths so my breathing wouldn't shake the box. Overhead, I felt the magics roiling together as they reacted to the other explosions. The air felt thick and heavy like the moment right before lightning and thunder strike at the same time. As soon as Heartsease exploded, the magics would whirl out of control. They would take the whole city with them, and I wouldn't be there to settle them again. Even if I was there, it might be too late.

Inside the box, the slowsilver had to be snailing out of the saucers toward the pile of tourmalifine crystals, drawn by the magic in Nevery's locus stone.

How much time did I have left? A quarter of an hour? A few minutes?

I rested my forehead against the wooden lid of the box. It was too late for anything. "Don't come, Nevery," I whispered. If he came now, he'd only arrive in time to be caught in the explosion. A crazy laugh trembled in my throat. Oh, wouldn't Nevery be annoyed when I blew up Heartsease again?

Then I heard a thump from downstairs.

I held my breath.

Another thump, and a rush of heavy footsteps on the stairs, and somebody threw the study door open.

Nevery strode into the room, Pip clinging to

his shoulder. Seeing me lashed to the box, he froze. "The fuse is set?"

"It's going to go off any second," I said. "You'd better get out of here."

Nevery snorted. "I don't think so, boy." Swiftly, he went to the shelves beside the table and found a penknife. Kneeling beside the box, he sawed at the rope tying my wrist to the handle. "I saw Crowe and his people getting into a boat outside," Nevery muttered to me. "But I didn't expect to find you here, my lad."

"You should have," I muttered.

"Hah," Nevery answered, and kept working on the ropes.

Pip dropped off Nevery's shoulder to the floor. The dragon edged closer to the box and sniffed at it.

"Don't bump the box," I whispered.

"Shh," Nevery said, and sawed through the last strand of rope. "Now the other hand." He got to his feet and made a wide circle around the box, then cut me free of the other handle.

I sat back and took a deep, trembling breath. Pip

swarmed up me to cling to my shoulder, panting.

"Now, get out," Nevery ordered.

What? "But I have to defuse the device," I said, getting shakily to my feet.

"No." Nevery pointed at the door. "It is my locus stone. I will do it."

But I was the one who'd stolen his stone! "No, Nevery!"

"Do as you're told for once, boy," he growled.

As an answer, I reached out and lifted the lid off the box.

Inside the box, silver-bright snails were flowing all over the blackpowder, coming closer and closer to the tourmalifine as they were drawn to the locus stone. Nevery stepped up beside me to see. We only had a second, maybe two.

We both started reaching for the stone. My hand trembled; Nevery's was steady. "You do it," I whispered.

Nevery didn't answer. Quick hands, steady hands, he reached into the box and plucked his locus stone from its nest of tourmalifine crystals.

At the same moment, attracted by the slowsilver, and by the magic in the stone, Pip leaped off my shoulder and into the box.

"Pip, *no*!" I shouted.

And then the world exploded.

CHAPTER

31

The roar of the explosion slammed into me and flung me out into the night. I tumbled through the darkness, and Pip flew next to me, tossed like a leaf in the wind. I saw Nevery, too, spinning away, surrounded by sparks and flames.

"Nevery!" I shouted, and reached out for him, but he was gone.

All around me, Heartsease burst apart, bricks and

chunks of wood and rooftiles and arrows of glass zinging past me and spiraling out into the night. A chimney sailed past, still trailing smoke, followed by the wooden table from Nevery's study, tumbling end over end. There went all the books from my room, flapping their pages like wings. And all around me, the magics whirled out of control, sweeping in wider and wider circles, sending wind and sparks lashing around the island.

Farther off, a rowboat plunged away, riding the whirlwind, and I saw Nimble, Sootle, and Crowe crouched, clinging to the sides of the boat.

Pip flashed past again, and I reached out and snatched the little dragon from the wind's grasp and pulled it to me.

"*Tallennar!*" I shouted, but I couldn't hear my own voice; the wind roared too loudly in my ears. A slate from the new roof grazed my ribs; a shard of glass cut a line of pain along one hand; I ducked as Nevery's favorite chair blundered past. I shoved Pip under my sweater for protection and looked wildly around for Nevery. He was tumbling farther and farther away.

I had my locus stone. No, I had two because I had Brumbee's stone in my pocket. And I had the power of a pyrotechnic explosion, and I could use it to demand the magics' attention. I had to do this before it was too late.

The magics rushed 'round the island again, making a towering vortex of sparks and thunder-clouds and lightning, gathering up all the splinters and bricks and ruin of Heartsease, spinning and wobbling like they were going to fly apart and shat-ter into a million pieces.

Gripping Brumbee's locus magicalicus, and clutching Pip, I shouted, as loud as I could in the dragon language, "*STOP.*"

I didn't really expect the magics to listen, but slowly, like an avalanche coming to rest, the mag-ics' wild whirling slowed, steadied. I could feel all of their power and attention fixed on me. They were upset and wild; they needed somebody to help them, or they would destroy the city.

"*Stop*," I told the magics again, and they spun down to a frozen silence. My feet thumped to the ground and I wobbled for a second and then found myself standing on the smooth-swept cobblestones of Heartsease island. The house was gone, and so was the black tree and all its birds. Beyond the island was only darkness. Above me, the magics waited, pressing down on me. So heavy.

I took a steadying breath. Pip crawled out from under my sweater and perched on my shoulder. I gripped Brumbee's locus magicalicus.

I gazed up into the tangled magics. The last time I'd tried this, the magics had almost taken me away. But I had to do it. The magics loomed like a towering storm, alive with thunder and lightning ready to strike. Slowly I spoke the words that would settle them again. It was like untangling one of Benet's snarls of wool—black strands all woven together, but once I got one strand unsnarled, another one would swirl into a new wild tangle. I shouted the spell louder, but my voice sounded tiny, disappearing in the huge rushing roar of the magics' winds. The magics grew heavier and heavier, bearing down on me. I pushed back, and the effort had me panting and seeing double and stumbling over the spellwords. On my shoulder, Pip drooped. The tendrils of magic wrapped around me, tighter and tighter. It was like trying to keep a huge boulder from falling off the edge of a cliff. It was about to go over, and take me with it. I fell to my knees.

I couldn't do this on my own. I needed help.

"Nevery!" I gasped. He was out there somewhere, caught up in the roiling magic overhead. "Magics," I ordered. "I need Nevery." I said it again, with all my strength, in the magic language. The magics knew him and his locus stone—they had to be able to bring him back.

A rushing sound, and "I am here, boy," Nevery's gravelly voice said from behind me. I jerked around and there he was, his hair and beard tangled, his feet settling onto the ground as if the magics had just set him there with a giant, invisible hand. "This is most interesting," he said, looking around.

"I need your help!" I panted.

"Ah." He bent and helped me to my feet. I swayed, and he put his hand on my shoulder, steadying me.

"Ready?" I asked, catching my breath.

"Yes, boy," Nevery said calmly, and held up his locus magicalicus.

I took a deep breath and spoke to the magics again, and Nevery spoke with me. Our voices boomed out together, and this time the magics listened. I untangled one bit of the magic and Nevery held it while I unsnarled another bit, and after a long, tiring time we had Arhionvar looming over the Sunrise and the old Wellmet magic spread like a warm blanket over the Twilight. There was a feeling like a deep sigh after a storm, and the magics clicked into place. There, settled. The city would be all right, at least for now.

And then, just as quickly as he'd come, Nevery

was gone from my side—the magics whirled him off, and he disappeared into the blackness.

"*No!*" I shouted.

They always wanted something in return, the magics. They'd taken my first locus stone, and they'd taken Heartsease, and they'd taken me, once. But they could *not* have Nevery.

"Give Nevery back!" I ordered the magics. "You can have Crowe instead. And Nimble and Sootle, too. But you have to give Nevery back!"

It was as if Arhionvar turned its huge, stony, uncaring back on me, ignoring my demand.

"Give him back!" I shouted. My voice sounded desperate and full of tears.

On its side of the river, the old Wellmet magic twinkled softly. Then, like the tide coming in, it washed up against Arhionvar's strength. I held my breath. "Please, magics," I whispered. "I helped you. Now I need your help."

Silence for a long, dark moment.

Then a stone fell out of the sky and landed next

to my foot. I flinched aside, then glanced at it. A brick.

Wait. A brick?

I blinked, and across the cobblestones from me, with a deafening *whumph*, the black-branched tree slammed out of the sky and back into the courtyard, its roots plunging into the ground. The cobblestones flowed out in a wave around the tree, knocking me to my knees again.

Bricks rained down all around me, piling themselves into walls. Wood arrowed out of the sky and arranged itself as floors. The chimney dropped into place, and the roof landed like a jaunty hat on top of it all. Windows slotted themselves into the walls, their glass flying in tinkling shards, then melting back into the frames. Books flew in the doorways and onto the shelves, and then the doors themselves bumped into place.

My feet settled onto the floor in Nevery's study. The wooden table thunked down next to me, and a last book found itself a place on the shelf. I reached out and touched the bricks of the fireplace. They felt solid and real.

"And Nevery, too?" I asked the magics.

Nothing, just silence. Tears started up in my eyes. I leaned my head against the cold bricks of the fireplace.

Please, magics. Please. Just give Nevery back and everything will be all right.

Then I heard a gruff cough and, "I am here, my lad."

I turned, and there he was, standing in the doorway. His beard looked a little singed, and he held to the doorframe to keep himself on his feet.

"Nevery?" I whispered.

He rubbed a sooty hand across his eyes, then smiled. "Yes, I believe so, boy."

CHAPTER 32

Rowan decided that the city needed a ceremony, with medals and speeches. We were in her office, me leaning against the wall by the door, Nevery sitting in one of the comfortable chairs, Rowan behind her desk, and Embre beside her in his wheeled chair. Pip was out hunting pigeons. Rowan had sent Miss

Dimity away so we wouldn't be interrupted.

Everybody in Wellmet knew bad things had been going on. They'd heard about the locus stone thieves, and the gangs in the Twilight and the Sunrise, and about the chimney swifts and Crowe coming back. All the city's people had felt the explosions and heard the fighting in the streets; they'd seen the ruins of Nimble's house and the Night Bridge, and they'd been frightened.

"A ceremony is a way of showing everybody that we're all right," Rowan said. "We tell the story about what happened, and then none of the magisters can blame you"—she pointed at me—"for stealing their locus stones, and my councilors can't whisper that you"—she smiled at Embre—"were secretly working with Crowe, or something stupid like that. Do you understand?"

Yes, I understood.

"I think," Embre said, "that at the ceremony I'll tell the part of the story about the duchess's bravery."

Rowan shot him one of her down-the-nose looks.

"What *are* you talking about?"

"That chimney swift would've killed me during the fight at Dusk House," Embre said, giving her a sharp grin. "You saved my life, Ro. Don't think I didn't notice."

She blinked. "I did, didn't I?" she said. She looked down at the desk as pink crept up into her cheeks.

I'd already explained to Rowan and Embre how, after Nevery and I had settled the magics, I'd gone back out to the courtyard to look at Heartsease, to be sure it was back to normal. On the cobblestones I'd found Crowe's clicker-ticker device, smashed into pieces. The magics had taken Crowe, that meant, and Nimble and Sootle, too, and with them gone forever, the city would be all right.

Now the Night Bridge was being rebuilt. Sandera and Trammel, the magisters whose stones had been destroyed in Nimble's pyrotechnic devices, were planning to leave the city, to travel and maybe look for new locus stones, though they weren't happy about it. With Rowan and Embre's new friendship, or whatever it was that had her blushing whenever he was around, and the two magics settled on each side of the river, the city was more stable than it'd ever been.

Except for me. I was still out of place. I still wasn't sure what I was.

For the two days since Crowe and Nimble had been defeated, I'd been staying in the ducal magister's rooms in the Dawn Palace. The servants were still afraid of me and Pip, and the rooms were still too grand, and the food was cold, and guards waited outside my doors anytime I wanted to go somewhere.

"What about you, Conn?" Rowan asked, interrupting my dark thoughts.

"What about me, what?" I asked back.

She gave me her sly, down-the-nose look. "At the ceremony, how shall we honor the ducal magister?"

Oh, not this again. "Ro, I am not the ducal magister," I said.

Ignoring my comment, Rowan glanced at Embre. "I think he should be awarded a medal."

Embre nodded. "A big, shiny one. And he'll have to give a speech, too."

I stared at them.

"Oh, yes," Rowan said, very solemnly. "A speech. A long one."

"I am *not*—" I started, and then Nevery gave a bark of laughter.

Rowan and Embre were laughing, too.

Oh.

Still smiling, Ro got up from behind her desk and came around to give me a hug. Then she stepped back and leaned against her desk. "What reward *do* you want, Conn?" Embre wheeled around to face me, too. Nevery, in his chair, was watching me and pulling at the end of his beard.

What did I want? Not medals and speeches, sure as sure. "Ro?" I asked.

"Connwaer," she said. Her lips twitched as if she was going to start laughing again.

"Well, Ro . . ." I tried again. Heartsease was my home, not the grand, damp, lonely Dawn Palace rooms.

Embre and Rowan exchanged a sparkling glance. "Oh, this must be important," Embre said.

I shot him a glare. Be quiet, Embre. Right. I took a deep breath. "Ro, I'm not a gutterboy, I know that. I can't live by myself in the Twilight anymore."

"Would you even want to?" she asked, quirking her eyebrows at me.

"No, not exactly," I answered. "I just . . . I don't . . ."

"It's hard for you to let anybody look after you, is that it?" my cousin Embre asked. "Because you looked after yourself for such a long time."

I nodded. "Yes, that's it." I took a deep breath. "And I can't live in the Dawn Palace. I'm not a gutterboy, but I'm not the ducal magister, either. I don't want any reward except to go home." I glanced over at Nevery, who nodded. "Back to Heartsease."

"Hm," Rowan said. "I'll consider it, Conn. On two conditions." She held up a finger. "One, you have to accept a reward." She reached behind her and picked up a clinking bag from her desk, and held it out. More money, to go with the other bag she'd given me.

"Some of that is from me," Embre put in. "You saved the Twilight part of the city too. Will you take it?"

I nodded, and Rowan handed me the bag of money. It was heavy. "What's the other thing?" I asked.

"The second condition," Rowan said, holding up two fingers. "Is this. If you're not the ducal magister, you'll have to decide what you are." She looked suddenly serious. "It's for the good of the city."

I nodded.

Rowan went on. "You are very powerful, Conn, and your power affects all of us. You don't fit properly into any category, and it makes a lot of people nervous, especially the magisters. We need to know what you are. Do you see what I'm talking about?"

I knew she was right. "Can I have some time to think about it?" I asked.

"You can," Rowan said. "And yes, you can do

your thinking in Heartsease."

My heart lifted. I grinned at her. "Thanks, Ro."

She grinned back, and suddenly she didn't seem duchessly at all. "You're welcome, Conn."

"Hmph," Nevery said gruffly, getting to his feet. "That's settled, then. Come along, boy. Let's go home."

After supper, we sat in the study drinking tea, Benet with his chair tilted back against the wall, knitting something with blue yarn, Nevery reading in a chair pulled up to the fireplace, and me sitting on the hearthstone. Lady-the-cat curled up next to me, purring. Pip sat on my shoulder with its tail around my neck like a scarf, asleep.

Suddenly, with a startling thump, Benet tipped all four legs of his chair back onto the floor. "More tea?" he asked, getting to his feet and setting his snarl of knitting on the table.

"Yes," Nevery said, still reading.

Instead of going down to the kitchen, Benet

waited until Nevery looked up from his book. "Tell him now, sir," Benet said, pointing at me. Without waiting for Nevery to answer, he went out, and I heard the sound of his footsteps thumping down the stairs.

Oh, right. Benet had said that Nevery had something to tell me.

"Well, boy," Nevery said, and then fell silent.

"Well, Nevery?" I asked. It couldn't be that important, not if he'd waited this long, whatever it was.

Nevery set his book aside and got up from his chair. Then he paced across the room to the table and back again. He folded his arms and looked down at me, where I sat on the hearthstone with Lady-the-cat and Pip. "Here it is, boy," he said gruffly. "I made a mistake sending you away from Heartsease. I missed you while you were gone, and I was worried when you ran away to the Twilight. The thing is . . ." He frowned, but I could see that he wasn't angry, it was something else. "It's this, boy.

This is your home. You know that."

"Yes," I said quietly.

Nevery sighed. "So apparently I must tell you the rest. It's this. You're as dear to me, Conn, as any son to his father."

I stared up at him. My lips moved as I whispered what he'd just said.

. . . *as any son to his father.*

"Yes, boy," Nevery said.

It hadn't been easy for him to say. It wasn't easy for me to say, either, because I wasn't used to it. But I said it. "I love you too, Nevery."

He smiled. "All well, boy?"

"Yes, Nevery," I said, grinning back at him. "All well."

"Good." He sat down again in his chair and picked up his book.

And that was that. We were settled, just like the city's magics.

After a while, Benet came in with the tea tray. He looked us over, then nodded and set the tray on the table with a clatter.

I got up and poured myself another cup of tea, then sat cross-legged on the hearthstone and set myself to thinking about Rowan's condition. If I wasn't the ducal magister, what was I, exactly? It made me remember when I'd first met Nevery, when I'd picked his pocket because the night was cold and empty and I hadn't had anything to eat since the day before. Back then I'd been just like the gutterkids and mudlarks and charkids. Now I had plenty to eat, and shelves full of books, and people who cared about me—who *loved* me, like father to son. And bags of money I didn't know what to do with.

"Nevery," I said. "D'you think I could—" I set down my teacup, thinking.

"What, boy?" Nevery said, looking up from his book.

"You know when I was a gutterboy?" I asked.

Nevery shook his head. "You never talk about that time."

I shrugged. "There's nothing to talk about. It was boring, mostly. I never thought about anything interesting." I glanced over at him. He was watching me with his keen-gleam eyes. "That's the thing, Nevery," I went on. "I was just a stupid gutterboy. I didn't even know how to read."

"You never had the opportunity to learn," Nevery said quietly.

No, I hadn't. "I would've wanted to," I said. I thought about it some more. The gutterkids and mudlarks and charkids. All they thought about was mudlarking or thieving or sweeping chimneys, and finding a warm place to sleep and enough to eat. None of them knew how to read. "Nevery, d'you think I could use the money I got from Rowan and Embre to help the gutterkids learn how to read?"

"You'd like to open a school?" Nevery leaned back in his chair, pulling on the end of his beard.

Hmmm. Maybe I did. I gazed into the fire. I didn't like people looking after me, and the mudlarks and the charkids and the other gutterkids in the Twilight were maybe the same way. They were used to being on their own. They didn't want anybody telling them what to do. But sometimes being looked after wasn't a bad thing. The gutterkids might come to a school to learn to read. They could have something to eat there, too, biscuits, maybe; that'd make them come, sure as sure. And they'd get warm now and then. I nodded. Yes, I wanted to start a school in the Twilight.

"It is a very good idea, Conn," Nevery said.

We sat for a few moments, watching the fire flicker in the fireplace and listening to the *click-click* of Benet's knitting needles.

"D'you know, Nevery," I said, realizing something. "I think I know what I am."

Nevery looked up from his book and raised his eyebrows.

"A wizard is nothing like a fine gentleman," I told him.

"Oh, indeed, boy?" he said with a snort.

Indeed, Nevery! I wasn't a fancy speech-giving,

meeting-attending, fine-gentleman wizard. The city didn't need a ducal magister like that, and neither did the magics. And I wasn't a ragged gutterboy, either. I was Nevery's boy, and I was friends with the duchess and the Underlord. Hmm. "The same way Rowan and Embre put the city first," I said, "I put the magics first."

Nevery nodded. "Yes, that is true."

I laughed. Oh, this was perfect. "Nevery, I'm supposed to look after the magics!"

I would be a new kind of ducal magister—the magics' magister. I would talk to the magics and protect them, and learn everything I could about them. I would help the old Wellmet magic settle into its place over the Twilight, and the stronger Arhionvar magic stay over the Sunrise. To do that I had to live in the middle of Wellmet, between the Sunrise and the Twilight, and that meant I would always stay right here in Heartsease with Nevery. The very center of the city.

Home.

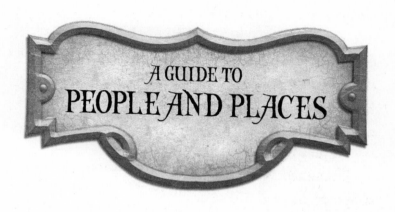

A GUIDE TO
PEOPLE AND PLACES

PEOPLE

BENET—A rather scary-looking guy, but one who loves to knit, bake, and clean. His nose has been broken so many times, it's been flattened. If he were an animal, he'd be a big bear. His hair is brown and sticks out on his head like spikes. You wouldn't want to meet him in a dark alley, but you would want to eat his biscuits.

CONNWAER—Has shaggy black hair that hangs down over his bright blue eyes. He's been a gutter-boy for most of his life, so he's watchful and a little wary; at the same time, he's completely pragmatic and truthful. He's thin, but he's sturdy and strong, too. He has a quirky smile (hence his quirked tail as a cat). Conn does not know his own age; it could be anywhere from twelve to fourteen. A great friend to have, but be careful that you don't have anything valuable in your pockets in reach of his sticky fingers.

EMBRE—The Underlord of the Twilight. A young man about nineteen years old. He is very thin and has a sharp face with dark eyes and black hair, and he might have smudges on his hands and face from working with blackpowder. Everything about him is sharp, including his intellect.

NEVERY FLINGLAS—Is tall with gray hair, a long gray beard, shaggy gray eyebrows, and sharp black eyes. He's impatient and grumpy and often hasty, but beneath that his heart is kind (he would never admit it). Mysterious and possibly dangerous, Nevery is a difficult wizard to read, but a good one to know.

NIMBLE—A magister and rather weak wizard. He looks like a bat and is a pen-pushing, officious man. He dislikes Conn very much.

 **PIP**—As Conn says, Pip is an "it," not a "he." Pip is a small dragon, no bigger than a kitten, but it has a very big attitude. Pip does not trust Conn at first—why should it? Conn stole it from its cave in the mountains, after all. Still, one thief should be friends with another. . . .

 **ROWAN FORESTAL**—The Duchess of Wellmet. A tall, slender girl of around sixteen, with red hair and gray eyes. She is very intelligent with a good, if dry, sense of humor.

PLACES

DAWN PALACE—The home of Rowan. The palace itself is a huge, rectangular building—not very architecturally interesting, but with lots of decorations crusted on it to make it fancy.

HEARTSEASE—The old Heartsease, the mansion house with the big hole in the middle, was destroyed in a certain pyrotechnic experiment, so Nevery is building a new Heartsease. When finished, it will have plenty of room for Nevery and Benet and Conn to live there. Conn might even get his own workroom!

MAGISTERS HALL—Seat of power for the wizards who control and guard the magic of Wellmet. It is a big, imposing gray stone building on an island with a wall built all the way around it at the waterline.

WELLMET RUNIC ALPHABET

In Wellmet, some people write using runes to stand for the letters of the alphabet. In fact, you may find some messages written in runes in *The Magic Thief: Home*.

a		l		tt	
b		ll		u	
bb		m		v	
c		mm		w	
d		n		x	
dd		nn		y	
e		o		z	
ee		oo			
f		p			
ff		pp			
g		q			
gg		r			
h		rr			
i		s			
j		ss			
k		t			

Uppercase letters are made by adding an extra line under a letter; for instance:

Uppercase A

Uppercase B

RUNIC PUNCTUATION:

Beginning of a sentence ·

End of a sentence (period) :

Comma ℯ

Question Mark ℈

The Magic Is Really Dragons
You need a more formal title than this, Connwaer.

A Paper About How the Magic Is Really Dragons
Look here, boy. If you expect to be taken seriously, you must begin with a serious title.

~~A Serious Paper on Seriously Dragon Magical Seriousness~~
Try this: A Disquisition on the Draconic Nature of Magic

A Disquisition on the Draconic Nature of Magic
All right, Nevery?   *Yes.*

                                    Duchies

For a long time, the wizards of the Peninsular ~~Duchys~~ thought that the magic in their cities welled up from the ground like water or gathered in one place because of the weather or unusual geological formations. The same wizards knew they needed to be holding a locus magicalicus to do magic, but they didn't know why. They used spoken spells, but they didn't think about what those words really meant. They saw that slowsilver attracted the magic, but they never figured out why it did. They also knew that the magic acted

388

strangely around pyrotechnics (when things blow up), but they didn't wonder about why that happened, either.

You know very well, boy, that most wizards want nothing to do with pyrotechnics.

I know, Nevery. But I'm not going to leave it out.

Those wizards figured magic was just a resource to be used, like some sort of sparkly cloud hanging over their cities. Basically they were completely wrong and (stupid) about magic.

Connwaer, you cannot say here that all of the wizards who lived for hundreds of years were wrong and stupid.

But they WERE stupid! If they'd only thought about it, they'd have figured it out long ago.

That may be so, but you cannot write it.

Basically they were completely and mistakenly wrong about magic. There's plenty of evidence to prove that the magics of each city are living beings that were once dragons or still are dragons, just in a different form. Four things make it clear as clear that this is true.

THE FIRST THING: DRAGON LANGUAGE

The first thing to consider is what magical spells really are. In the past, the ~~stupid~~ *mistaken* wizards thought the magical spells were just words that when spoken aloud focused the wizard's mind so he or she could cast the spell. These mistaken wizards thought they were DOING magic. Really, we wizards don't DO magic at all, we just ask the magic to do things for us. For example, when wizards use the spellword *lothfalas*, we are not making light, we are asking the dragon-magic to make light for us, which it always does. *I assume you will explain why the dragon-magic performs the wizard's requests?*

I'm not sure I can explain it, Nevery.

When we wizards seem to be doing powerful magic, then, we are really just speaking another language to a giant being a lot more powerful than we are.

Perhaps, Conn, you could compare this transformation to what happens when a butterfly sheds its cocoon.

THE SECOND THING: SLOWSILVER

Good idea.

When a magic-dragon is small, it looks like an ordinary dragon with colorful scales. The scales are really like a shell covering the real dragon, the magic, which is inside the scales. As a dragon ages, it grows larger, and when it is huge—the size of the top of a mountain or a city—it transforms. Its scales turn silver with age and then drop away, and the magical being inside is released. The magic that emerges is still dragon—it is still a living thing—it's just in a new form, one that stays in one place because the slowsilver scales that once confined it have pooled in that place and keep it settled there. In Wellmet, the slowsilver flowed into the river that runs through the city and is hidden under the water. We can't see it, but the slowsilver is there, anchoring the city's magic to this specific place.

If somebody were to take all the slowsilver out of a city, the magic would leave that place, too, which is what happened in Desh with the slowsilver mines. The Desh magic-dragon was weakened and almost cut off from its city when so much of the slowsilver keeping it there was mined and sold to other places. Now the people who live in the city of Desh are buying up the slowsilver they sold off before, and the magic-dragon is settling there again.

THE THIRD THING: LOCUS STONES

It's well known that dragons hoard precious jewels. That's only partly right—a dragon hoards lots of different kinds of ordinary stones and rocks, and only some of them are jewels. When a dragon changes into its magic-dragon form, it is still attracted to the stones and jewels that were once part of its hoard. Basically a locus magicalicus is a fancy name for any kind of stone that happened to be part of a dragon's hoard.

Really, wizards aren't any different from any other people. Wizards don't have any special talents. Wizards are regular people who have found a locus magicalicus, so the magic can sort of hear them when they speak the dragon language.

Conn, many of your readers will be angered by this claim.

I know. But it's still true.

There remains the fact that locus stones do call to specific people, as your jewel stone did. How do you explain that?

I do know that the magic chose me but not because I'm special or have any amazing talent, but because it wanted me to do something for it. Maybe it knew that I didn't have anybody looking out for me, so I'd be free to do the things it needed me to do. Maybe the magic always matches its hoarded stones to the people it thinks most likely to help it.

So you're saying that wizards act in the world on behalf of the magics?

I think so. Sometimes. I have to think about this some more. Maybe we serve them, and they serve us at the same time.

Maybe so. Fascinating.

THE FOURTH THING: PYROTECHNICS

Even though the magics in their dragon forms look a lot like giant lizards, they aren't cold-blooded like lizards, they are warm. Even their scales are warm. *Perhaps you should add here that you know this from personal experience.*

The dragons that I have seen are warm. They breathe fire, and their breath smells like fireworks. Maybe pyrotechnics remind the magics of their former dragon-shaped selves, because when explosions go off in their cities, the magics get very, very interested, and sometimes even upset.

Nevery, should I put in here how I used pyrotechnics to talk to the Wellmet magic?

No. Save it for another disquisition.

Another one!?

CONCLUSION

Why should such a mighty creature as a dragon serve us, the human wizards who live in their cities? It's sure as sure a good question. The answer is that the dragon-magics don't serve us. To them, we are tiny creatures—the dragons don't even notice most humans, only the ones holding a locus stone and speaking their language (wizards), or getting their attention with explosions (pyrotechnists). We exist to them only as one part of a city, though a warmer, more welcoming part. They like having us in their cities because we keep them company, in a way, and so they protect us, and help us when we ask nicely.

Connwaer, this paper is going to get you into a good deal of trouble.

That's all right, Nevery. Trouble is what I'm best at.

Hah. And maybe that, boy, is why the magic of Wellmet chose you.

Conn—

The palace cook reports that you ate none of the dinner I had sent to your ducal magister rooms last night. This astonishes me, as I know how completely <u>obsessed</u> you are on the subject of food. I do want you to feel at home here at the palace, so choose what you like best from this menu, and the cook will prepare it for you.

—Rowan

De- *Appetizers* Things to make you lose your appetite, this means.

Cold collation of pickled beetroot and salted ⟨marrow⟩

Marrow is the inside of bones, Ro. Bones.

Roasted newt

Sheep soup Too woolly for me.

Fish and horseradish chowder

Three squeaks with salt sauce

I can't even eat one squeak.

Raw peppered garlic-onion dainties

*Fermented chicken liver niblets served with
crackers and a parsley garnish*

Blood sausage on rye toast roundels
Does blood sausage really have blood in it?

Main Dishes

*I don't want
to know what a
chitterling is.*

??

*Kidney and boiled chitterlings in gelatin served
over chilled buckwheat noodles*

Deep-fried snout stuffed with turnip jelly

*I know what snout is.
It's nose.* *Potted meat served in a pool
of celery cream* *Sure as sure, this is horrible
meat-like bits smashed together.*

*Pickled egg with cold shredded cabbage
and iced mint jelly* *Brrrr.*

*Could I have the
fritter without the* *Cockle fritters in licorice sauce*
cockle or the sauce?

Cabbages and potatoes with butter ~~tongue gravy~~

Sweets

White flour-jelly with raisins

Ro, I hate raisins.

Suet sponge cake with raisins

Mincemeat slab *With raisins, I'm guessing.*

Savory jam pastry with raisin sauce

With flies is more likely, if it's from the Twilight. Twilight custard with raisins

Petrified pudding with dried ~~raisins~~ *flies*

Ro, biscuits are easy—could I have some of those, with butter? And a pot pie, but one with no liver or tongue or snout or chitterlings or any other mysterious meat parts in it? I'll eat that other stuff if I have to, but it's not anything that Benet would cook at home.

THANKS TO...

Loads of thanks to this novel's first readers: Greg van Eekhout, Jenn Reese, Ingrid Law, Robin LaFevers, Deb Coates, Lisa Bradley, and Dorothy Winsor. Wow, there are a lot of you.

To my genius editor, Antonia Markiet, and her editorial assistant, Abbe Goldberg. And the always-outstanding publishing team at HarperCollins Children's: publisher Susan Katz, editor-in-chief Kate Jackson, senior production editor Kathryn Silsand, senior art director Amy Ryan, senior designer Tom Forget, and production manager Esilda Kerr.

To my agent, Caitlin Blasdell, of the Liza Dawson Associates literary agency.

To readers Edie Parsons, for getting Benet together with Captain Kerrn, Toby Barnes, for the extra bacon, and Tasha Kazanjian and Nancy Fink.

To my mom for the eggplant surprise.

Ingrid, we have to try again for lunch!

And thanks to all my dear families, especially my mom and dad and the memory of my dear old Sparks-like grandma, Anne Hudson Hankins.

Don't miss a moment of this enchanting fantasy-adventure series.